"Did anyone s

here?" Luke asked

"No." Meg quickly stepped inside and leaned against the door.

"Thank God! Those reporters are everywhere." A slow smile came to his lips. "Then nobody knows you're here?"

Her heart thundered in her chest. "That's right."

"Oh, Meg." He sighed and caressed her cheeks with his thumbs.

If I let him kiss me, I'm done for. He took her by the hand and led her into the suite. One kiss and then she'd go. This would be the last time she'd kiss Luke.... Her thoughts ceased as his lips touched hers with such intense passion that it left her shaking.

"Don't go," he murmured, his lips moving to her throat. "No one has to know. Surely we deserve this much."

"All I know is how much I need you."

"You have me, Meg. You always have." With a growl, he scooped her up and carried her through the bedroom door.

Dear Reader,

I threw out all my previous ideas about researching a book when it came to LOVERBOY. I'd expected to hang around the Chandler, Arizona, Ostrich Festival taking notes and smiling. Oh, no. I barely had a chance to watch one ostrich race (they're a total riot) before the gregarious people of Chandler had me running errands, hawking soda, even riding in the parade! (That was the treat to end all treats. My parade vehicle was a car to die for—a burgundy Corvette convertible.)

In the process of working the festival, I learned what Chandler's volunteers already knew—the comradery, coupled with the satisfaction of raising money for a good cause, makes the broken fingernails, aching backs and hoarse throats all worth it.

By the end of the three-day festival I was exhausted, but this year I'll be back, plunging willingly into the chaos again. This time I'll be selling my book, which will be used as an additional fund-raiser. I'm proud that the good folks of Chandler want to include me.

Sincerely,

Vicki Lewis Thompson

LOVERBOY

VICKI LEWIS THOMPSON

Harlequin Books

TORONTO • NEW YORK • LONDON
AMSTERDAM • PARIS • SYDNEY • HAMBURG
STOCKHOLM • ATHENS • TOKYO • MILAN
MADRID • WARSAW • BUDAPEST • AUCKLAND

For Carol Albrecht Shutt, whose suggestions and friendship propelled this book into existence.

I also gratefully acknowledge the help of Lori Daniels, Mary Ellen Crane and all the wonderful people of Chandler who made me feel a part of their special community.

ISBN 0-373-25584-5

LOVERBOY

This edition published by arrangement with Harlequin Enterprises B. V.

Printed in U.S.A.

1

A CHANDELIER SPRINKLED with rainbows dominated the elegant room where Sheila stood waiting, her eyes wide, her breathing rapid. Luke's glance settled hungrily on the rise and fall of her creamy breasts barely contained by the plunging neckline of her black silk dress.

He crossed the room in three strides and pulled her into his arms. The silk rustled against the stiff denim of his jeans. "Now, we'll settle this." He gazed into her upturned face. He didn't love her, but that didn't matter. As he had so many times before, he'd pretend she was Meg. His voice was low, urgent. "You know what I want."

"I can't give you that anymore!"

A muscle twitched in his jaw as desire pounded through his body. "Then I'll just have to take it." Ignoring her protests, he crushed his mouth against hers.

"Cut!"

MEG TOOK A DEEP BREATH and reached for the phone; her hands shaking as she punched in Didi's number. While she waited for her friend to answer, she glanced at the stack of posters propped against the desk of her home office. A cartoon version of a long-lashed ostrich advertised the Chandler Ostrich Festival only two weeks away.

Her gaze traveled to a box of silk-screened ostrich festival T-shirts in one corner of the room before roaming over the festival paperwork littering every available surface. Festival brochures and advance news clips covered the bulletin board over her desk, along with a lapel pin announcing Meg O'Brian as Board Member, Chandler Chamber Of Commerce.

Didi answered on the fourth ring. Meg and Didi had been friends since third grade, so there was no need for Meg to identify herself. "The TV network just called." Meg's stomach was churning. "They've chosen our parade grand marshal."

"And?"

"Luke Bannister."

"I'll be damned. The return of Chandler's favorite son."

"Right. The drag-race king of Arizona Avenue. The guy who appeared on stage smashed out of his mind for the school musical and turned a skunk loose during graduation."

"I doubt those things are in his press release. But don't panic. It'll be okay. Would you believe he has a local fan club?"

"What?"

"I'm only slightly embarrassed to tell you I'm in it."

"Didi, you're not!"

"I know you don't watch the soaps, but you really should tune in to *Connections.* Trust me, one episode with Luke as Dirk Kennedy and you'd be hooked."

"I don't *want* to be hooked. I—"

"For goodness' sake, Meg. It's only harmless fantasy."

Maybe for you, Meg thought. *Luke didn't break your heart.*

"When's he coming in?" Didi asked. "As parade chairperson I should confirm the presidential suite at the San Marcos and arrange for a limo at the airport."

"You can cancel the suite. He's staying with his brother."

"I guess he and Clint must've patched up their feud. When should I schedule the limo?"

"Well—" Meg's pulse raced as the full impact of Luke's visit hit her "—for some reason, he sent word that I'm supposed to pick him up."

"You're kidding!"

"He probably just wants to brag about his accomplishments."

"That would fit the Luke we all knew and loved. Be careful, toots. If he tries to stir the embers, you'd be in deep—"

"I'm not that stupid. Besides, I can't believe he's interested in me, after years of dating starlets."

"Maybe not, but be careful, anyway."

"I will. And as long as I have you on the phone, I have a couple of questions about the parade." As they talked, Meg forced her attention away from Luke, but every so often her heart repeated a reminder that he was coming back, like a news bulletin along the bottom of a television screen. They hadn't spoken in ten years, and their last words had been bitter. The ride from the airport to the Bannister cotton farm could be a long trip if Luke spent the time boasting about his success.

"Listen, Meg, *Connections* is almost on," Didi said. "Maybe you should take a look and familiarize yourself with Luke's character, in case the media ask you questions about the show."

"Uh...okay." Meg's stomach pitched. She'd avoided the show on purpose, figuring there was no use in summoning the ghost of old passions.

"You're probably the only person in Chandler who hasn't seen it at least once. You'd better watch it, if only to make sure you recognize Luke at the airport."

"Right. Bye, Didi." There wasn't a chance in hell she'd mistake Luke at the airport. Sometimes, in her dreams, she still saw his eyes. Like a sailor walking the plank, she left her office, strode into the living room and turned on the television.

The episode opened with a scene between two women named Sheila and Daphne, who had an argument Meg couldn't follow. During the commercial break Meg drew a deep breath and lounged back on her green plaid sofa. Luke probably wasn't even on today's show.

Suddenly, there he was. She leaned forward as the blood sang in her ears and her skin prickled. There he was.

He paused in the doorway of an ornate room lit by a crystal chandelier. His hair was a little shorter than he'd worn it in high school, but it still fell dark and untamed over his forehead. The extravagant set made his worn jeans and denim shirt look roguish by contrast.

He gazed purposefully at Sheila. Meg's pulse quickened. She remembered that look, the blatant sexuality in those blue eyes. Oh, God, how she remembered.

Then he crossed the room. His walk brought a familiar pang of longing. He moved with a loose-hipped stride that seemed to announce he knew exactly where he was going. When he reached for Sheila, Meg almost stopped breathing.

As they kissed, Meg spun back through time. She'd written an ode to Luke's kiss and then burned it in a teacup; her tears had helped put out the tiny fire. It made no sense that she could feel the anguish still, but the pain of her first heartbreak had seared deep, creating a scar she would carry forever.

The scene ended and a commercial flashed on. Meg sat in a daze, not looking at the TV. All she could see was the image of the first man she'd ever loved. And he was coming home.

TWO WEEKS LATER on Wednesday afternoon, Meg stood in the terminal of Phoenix's Sky Harbor Airport and tried to keep her cool. Luke's plane had just landed. Any minute now he'd walk through the dark passageway and she'd be face-to-face with the man who'd haunted her dreams for the past two weeks. She'd come alone as he'd requested, although back in Chandler preparations were under way for an elaborate welcoming celebration.

She'd been in an ornery mood since early morning, when she'd rejected the business suit she'd planned to wear in favor of worn jeans and a forest green knit pullover. Luke would probably arrive in some Hollywood glitz outfit, but she wouldn't play the game of one-upmanship with him. As her rebellious mood had blossomed, she'd decided to drive her twenty-year-old green truck to the airport instead of the silver BMW she and Dan had bought two years ago. Let Luke parade his success before her and appear gauche for doing so. Let him be embarrassed for a change.

The door to the jetway opened and passengers filed out. Meg scanned the group, comparing each person who appeared with the man who'd been on her television screen for the past two weeks. She'd secretly watched every episode of *Connections*, searching for things to hate about Luke. Her search had produced mixed results. His character on the show was arrogant and ruthless, traits she could despise, but Dirk Kennedy was also as sexy as hell. Of course, on the show he'd had the benefit of makeup artists and wardrobe consultants. He couldn't possibly look as magnetic in person as he did on screen.

She hadn't counted on him looking better.

When he walked into the terminal wearing formfitting jeans and a tight blue T-shirt, Meg gripped the back of a waiting-area chair to steady herself. If he'd been handsome in high school, he was magnificent now. Dammit.

He had a garment bag slung over one shoulder and a small duffel bag in his other hand. The harsh fluorescent lights of the terminal couldn't destroy the impact of his square jaw, his sculpted mouth, his prominent cheekbones. His walk, his gaze, even his grip on the duffel bag projected sexual power. Meg saw several women stare at him. Two women glanced his way and talked excitedly to each other. Meg decided she'd better get him out of the terminal before somebody recognized him. Or perhaps that was what he wanted.

She waved. He spotted her and smiled, but before either of them could move, a camera flashed. Meg glanced at the photographer, a scruffy young woman in baggy shorts and tank top, with a Dodgers baseball cap on backward. She had a second camera slung across her chest like a bandolier, and she snapped off shots as if firing a weapon. Meg had never seen paparazzi before, but the commando tactics of the young woman suggested she was one of that tenacious breed. Her flurry of activity drew more people, and Luke was quickly surrounded.

As Meg wondered what to do next, the knot of people began edging in her direction. She backed up a step before realizing that the group was moving toward her simply because Luke was.

"You'll have to excuse me, but I'm due in Chandler and I wouldn't want to disappoint the people waiting for me," he said, lifting his voice over the crowd.

He must relish announcing he had a whole town at his beck and call, she thought. His tone had deepened in ten years, but Meg recognized the same voice that had spoken words of love in the back of a pickup truck. The same voice that later had told her to get lost.

He'd put his duffel bag on the floor and was scribbling autographs on ticket envelopes and napkins. The young woman with the camera contorted her body to get shot after shot. "Dirk, aren't you afraid Sheila's husband is going to find out about you?" a woman on the fringe of the crowd called out.

Meg was startled by the question until she figured out that the woman thought Luke really *was* Dirk Kennedy and that he was actually carrying on an affair with Sheila behind her husband's back.

Luke didn't seem confused at all. He smiled at the woman who'd asked the question. "Sheila and I are very discreet. Besides, her husband keeps his nose in the *Wall Street Journal* all the time. The man has tons of money and no imagination. He'll never guess." The crowd laughed, but Meg's jaw tightened at the arrogance he displayed. "Well, gotta go." Luke flashed the same naughty-little-boy smile he'd used to such effect on the show. "Got another beautiful woman waiting for me."

Meg recoiled. How dare he lump her in with his bevy of conquests? The patronizing so-and-so! The crowd and the photographer immediately turned their attention on her and she shrank back in dismay.

"Sheila will be jealous!" someone shouted. *Flash, flash* went the camera.

"Sheila doesn't ever have to know, does she?" Luke picked up his bag, transferred it to the same hand that held his garment bag and winking, put his free arm around Meg. "Let's go," he urged in an undertone. "Hustle that little butt of yours."

"You mean run?" She was seeing spots from the camera's flash and she flinched from his invasion of her space. His touch was the same. Even his scent was the same. Her memory had lost nothing in ten years.

"Yes, run. Pretend we just stole oranges from old man Peterson's tree."

"If you say so." Meg took a deep breath and grasped her purse firmly.

"Now." Luke squeezed her shoulder and released his grip. They sprinted forward, catching the group surrounding them by surprise. They reached the elevators leading to the parking garage, and by a stroke of luck, the doors of one slid open in front of them. They dashed in.

Panting, Meg turned to him. "Any more luggage?"

"This is it." He grinned at her. "Out of shape, are we?"

She noticed he wasn't even breathing hard. "Some of us don't have personal trainers," she snapped.

"There was a day when you could run a mile without even getting winded, and with a load of oranges tied in the hem of your T-shirt besides."

"Then apparently I haven't aged as well as you."

His smile faded and his gaze traveled over her. "I wouldn't say that. You look great, Meg."

She flushed, and hated herself for doing it. She had a master's degree in political science and a responsible position in the community. Why was she reacting to his compliment like a love-struck teenager? "Thank you," she said, regarding him with what she hoped was calm indifference. When the elevator doors opened she led the way into the tiered parking garage and hoped to hell she could remember where she'd parked.

"What'd you bring?"

"My truck." She waited for his snort of derision. None came.

"You don't mean Kermit?"

She nodded. *Now all I have to do is figure out where I put him.*

"That's great. Is he still green?"

"New paint job, but he's still green." She squinted down the row of vehicles in one direction. Then, trying to appear nonchalant, she gazed in the other.

Luke began to laugh. "Same old Meg. I can remember roaming the parking lot at school, looking for your truck."

"I've gotten much better." *Except today.*

"Are we on the right level?"

"Yes."

"Then let's start walking."

Feeling like a dope, she fell into step beside him. "You must wonder how I'm running an entire community festival if I can't even remember where my truck is parked."

"I don't wonder at all. You were always a whiz at organizing things. Usually you had so much on your mind you'd be thinking of details while you robotted your way through the ordinary stuff, like parking. Of course you'd forget where you put your truck."

"That's a very nice rationalization," she said primly.

"Isn't this it, right here?"

She looked where he pointed and felt warmth rising in her cheeks once more. She'd almost walked right past the darn thing. "Yes, that's it."

"Boy, does this bring back memories." Luke put his hand on the tailgate. "Remember when I made that romantic remark that your truck matched your eyes?"

The comment jolted her and she glanced away. "Not really." He had a lot of nerve bringing that up, as if he thought they could laugh about it together. Their first real date, and she'd had to drive because his license was still suspended from his latest drag-racing incident. He'd told her that her truck matched her eyes, and then he'd kissed her. A transforming kiss, one that awakened needs she'd never known existed until his lips caressed hers.

He heaved his luggage into the back of the truck. "It was on our first date." He glanced back at her, as if prompting her to remember.

She shook her head and forced a gay laugh. "Goodness, that was *so* long ago." She avoided meeting his eyes as she hurried to unlock the passenger door. "We'd better get going. The welcoming committee is waiting for you."

After navigating the concrete ramps of the garage, Meg paid the parking fee while batting away Luke's offer of money. He wasn't going to pull the big spender routine on *her*.

"This ostrich festival sure was news to me," Luke said as they drove away from the airport. "Do you really draw a crowd of two hundred thousand?"

"Last year we did. It's the chamber's biggest fundraiser. We got the idea because they used to raise ostriches here, back when there was a market for ostrich plumes."

"Yeah, I read that in the publicity package they sent me. But I've been having a lot of trouble picturing an ostrich race."

"They're trained to run, after a fashion, anyway. The company who brings them in has camel and llama races, too. And we arrange for the other stuff you'd expect, like a carnival, food booths, entertainment."

"Carnival?" His tone was teasing. "Do you personally check out the rides?" When she shook her head, he laughed. "Didn't think so. You always were a chicken about heights." His constant references to their shared history were unnerving. She wouldn't have thought he'd want to dredge up the past this way, because if he kept it up, eventually they'd come to the unpleasant parts. "I was surprised at the band you got for Saturday night," he said. "Real headliners. There was a time I would've given anything to play with those guys."

"But now you wouldn't?"

"Actually I still would give a lot. I haven't touched my guitar in a long time, and I miss playing. But my schedule's so tight—"

"I'm sure it is," she cut in, trying to forestall a recitation of his important, busy schedule.

He shifted his gaze away. Then he rolled down the window and stuck out his head. "Hey! Look at that sky. And the air doesn't smell like smelly socks, either. Good, clean air."

"Except when they're ginning cotton." She really was in a perverse mood.

"Oh, yeah. That is pretty gross. You know, in some ways I feel as if a century has gone by since I lived in

Chandler. But then in other ways, like tooling along the road with you in this old truck, it seems as if I never left."

"The scene at the airport should have convinced you that everything's changed."

Luke grimaced. "It's that photographer. She must have been on the plane. I think she's just a kid working on her first celebrity, and I'm it. She's looking for a compromising shot, so she'll be hanging around a lot, unfortunately."

"Are you going to give her one?"

"I don't plan to." Looking back, he breathed a sigh of relief. "Thank God, she's not following us yet. She probably had to rent a car. She obviously hasn't learned all the tricks yet." He glanced at the dashboard. "Does your radio still work?"

"Yes."

"Got it on KNIX?"

"Yes." So some things hadn't changed. Luke still liked country music. When he switched on the radio, Garth Brooks was crooning an old favorite about being glad he didn't know how it all would go, how it all would end. Meg figured that would be a good philosophy for the next five days. She didn't want to know the outcome.

"So it's Meg O'Brian now."

"That's right." She tensed. Now the questions would begin.

"I guess you found yourself an Irishman. That must have pleased your folks."

She glanced at him. "Yes."

"But you're not wearing a ring. Is that some sort of feminist statement?"

He'd certainly been observant in the short time he'd been with her. She delivered her explanation with a certain grim satisfaction, glad to take him down a peg. "I don't wear a wedding ring because Dan was killed in a car accident two years ago."

"Oh, God." He looked away, staring at the freeway traffic. "Meg, I'm sorry."

"So am I."

"I feel like such a jerk. All I heard from the network was that Meg Hennessy O'Brian was running the festival. I thought you'd have a husband, maybe some kids.... I'm sorry. Me and my big mouth."

She felt a stab of pity for his obvious distress. "It's been two years now. The pain's not as bad." She paused and the music from the radio filled the silence. "Clint must not be a very good source of information."

"No. But that's not all his fault. I ticked him off pretty good when I didn't come home for Dad's funeral last summer."

"A lot of people didn't understand that."

"Did you?"

She hesitated. She didn't want to be his friend. After all, he hadn't been hers at the end of their relationship. But she couldn't forget the bruises Orville Bannister had left on him. She might be the only one who had known. "I understood," she said.

"That's good." He sighed and settled back against the seat. "I wanted to be there for Clint, but I didn't think I could stomach the funeral, with everybody making pious statements about Dad. Clint and I never did agree about our old man."

"But you're staying with Clint this weekend. Things must be better between you two now."

"I guess. The network notified him I'd be coming."

"You didn't call him?"

"I tried, but I never seemed to catch him at home. Probably out with some woman."

"Debbie Fry."

Luke chuckled. "I see Chandler's still a small town, even if the population figures say different."

"It's a good town, Luke."

"You're happy here, then."

"Yes, I am."

"Makes sense. You always belonged. Chandler and I never were a good fit. After being away, I can see it more clearly than ever. I can appreciate the good things about the place, but I could never live here again. Never."

Meg fell silent. His complete rejection of the town she loved, the town she planned to live in forever, felt like a slap. But what had she expected from a big important star like Luke Bannister? Some announcement that he planned to make Chandler his weekend home? Apparently she'd been watching too many soap operas.

2

A WIDOW. As he'd fantasized about this meeting he'd often dreamed that she was divorced, or unhappily married, and he'd rush to the rescue. But he'd never imagined this, wouldn't have wanted it for her. Poor Meg. The thought of her grief tore at him. But underneath his shock lurked a thought he was almost ashamed of . . . she was free. And frosty as hell. Undoubtedly she still nursed a grudge, which wasn't all bad. Anger was better than indifference.

Now that they were on Chandler Boulevard, she drove with her window down, the breeze blowing her long hair back from her face. He remembered her hair had been nearly white when she was little, but now it had deepened to the color of the Cracker Jack popcorn they used to eat.

In preparation for this trip, he'd told himself she might be fat; she might be pregnant; she might be oblivious to him. She was none of these. Her awareness of him was a palpable thing—just as it had been ten years ago, when he'd figured out what love was all about. Then, as now, it was all about Meg.

Surreptitiously he studied her as they drove. She still had that open, fresh-scrubbed face that reminded him of the models in an Eddie Bauer catalog. But an element of mystery had been added through her marriage, her widowhood. Ten years ago he'd imagined he knew everything about her. Now he was missing the most elemental knowledge of all, and he felt illogically cheated.

"Everything sure has changed," he said, breaking the silence between them.

She nodded. "The population's about five times bigger than when you left. You can see the evidence along this road."

He hadn't really been talking about Chandler, but he'd allow her to misunderstand him for the time being. In keeping with that, he looked obediently out the window at the fast-food restaurants, shopping centers and high-tech business plazas lining the street that had once bisected open fields. At least the familiar San Tan Mountains east of town hadn't changed. At four thousand feet, they weren't the "purple mountain majesties" he'd sung about in school, but he liked them, anyway. They had a coziness about them, as if a giant had spilled a huge box of brown sugar across the desert floor.

They passed what he was sure had been his and Meg's old make-out road. Once a dirt lane bordering an irrigation ditch, it was now a paved drive skirting a warehouse. A half mile or so down the road a cottonwood tree had towered forty feet in the air. On summer nights bits of fluff from the tree had floated down and drifted over their half-clothed bodies like snow. The tree was gone, but the memory made him ache with the same ferocity as when he'd been eighteen.

How he'd suffered on those nights when they'd spread a blanket in the back of his pickup and made out, doing just about everything except intercourse. He'd even brought condoms along one night, but hadn't used them. At the last moment he'd decided he and Meg should wait until they were married—one of the few decisions he could be proud of in his youth.

"I guess I ought to warn you about something," Meg said.

"What?"

"Instead of the keys to the city, the chamber is presenting you with a male ostrich."

"Excuse me?"

"A young male ostrich. Still pretty much a baby. He's the mascot for this year's festival."

"Ho, boy. Just what I've always wanted."

"He's named Dirk Kennedy, after your character in *Connections*."

Luke groaned. "Here it comes. I suppose because he struts around."

"That, and the fact that male ostriches keep at least three females at one time. This one hasn't gone through puberty yet, so you don't have to worry that he'll start chasing the chicks, so to speak."

Luke had to smile at the tartness with which she delivered that speech. "An ostrich. What am I supposed to do with it?"

"Pose. And watch out for its beak. They love to peck at anything shiny."

"Well, I don't have on anything shi—" He glanced down at his button fly where metal fasteners winked up at him. "Uh-oh."

"Maybe the welcoming ceremony will be short."

"I can guarantee it." As they approached the center of town, Luke's eyes widened. "My God, look at all this."

"That's the Rocky Mountain Bank Center. Most of the storefronts on the square have been remodeled to blend in with it and the exterior of the San Marcos Hotel."

Arizona Avenue had been widened, and a grassy mall added. He gazed at the lush greenery and fountains, the turquoise metal canopy arching over the street. But mostly he noticed the crowd of about one hundred people gathered in front of the peach-colored building on their left, the new bank building. "Everyone's here because of me?"

"That's right."

Then he saw the ostrich. Dirk Kennedy stood about five feet tall from feet to beak. As they drew closer, he could see the black-feathered body and stubby white feathers that would eventually be plumes. It had to weigh at least two hundred pounds. A man was holding it on a leash, but Luke didn't believe for a moment that the man could control that bird if it decided to bolt. "Good Lord."

"The ostrich is pretty tame. It was hand-raised," Meg said.

"I'll bet that took a lot of hands. Meg, who are all these people? Is that the pep band?"

"The pep band, which is delighted to get out of school to welcome you, plus the members of the Luke Bannister Fan Club, some of whom asked for time off work to be here, the mayor and his wife, the chamber president and his wife and most of my committee heads for the festival, many of whom are also members of your fan club, I discovered recently."

"I expected the network to send a crew for publicity purposes, but this is amazing."

"Nobody wanted to miss your arrival. By the way, a rental car's been following us for the past three miles. I expect your eager photographer's in it." She pulled the truck over to the curb and the pep band struck up the Chandler High School Wolves' fight song.

Luke took a deep breath. Whoever said you can't go home again? he thought. You can go anytime you want, but you have to be prepared. They might be waiting for you with a five-foot ostrich. "Okay, Meg. Let's do it."

MEG WATCHED HIM go into action. He climbed down from the truck with a brilliant smile and a big wave befitting his star status. The old Luke, the one she'd fallen in love with, would have begged her to get him out of here. The new sophisticated Luke had learned to face the music, which had now become a jazzed-up version of the theme song from *Connections*.

But, even the pep band couldn't drown out the cries and squeals of the fan club. Meg rolled her eyes at the crowd of women waving signs that said We Love You, Luke, and Dirk Kennedy For President. Some people had no shame, she thought.

She spotted Didi standing with her husband, Chuck, and watched as they sidled up to Luke like long-lost friends. During the months Meg had dated Luke, he'd been accepted by her crowd, which had included Chuck and Didi. After he'd dumped her, they had given him the cold shoulder, but she could hardly expect her friends to snub him now, ten years later. She couldn't expect it, but she did wish Didi had been a little less enthusiastic, for loyalty's sake.

Gradually Luke made the rounds of well-wishers, shaking hands with the men and accepting single red roses from the women. At last he came to Joe Randolph, who was holding the ostrich. The mayor, Keith Garvey, stood beside Joe. When Luke reached them, Keith signaled to the pep band for silence.

"Luke Bannister, you have made your hometown proud of you," he announced, "and we appreciate your presence at our annual ostrich festival more than we can say." The TV cameraman moved in. The mayor smiled. "Perhaps this will be some indication of our gratitude. We've named the festival mascot after your character in *Connections*. We've got him on a leash, because if he lives up to his namesake, he's liable to go after every female ostrich within a hundred miles."

The crowd laughed and the women from the fan club whooped in approval. "May I present," the mayor continued, "Dirk Kennedy." He handed the leash to Luke as the crowd whistled and cheered.

"I don't know when I've ever been so moved," Luke said, warily accepting the leash.

Meg couldn't help noticing he held his bouquet of flowers over his crotch. Cameras whirred as Luke made a little speech about the honor of being the festival's grand marshal. The scruffy young woman had alighted from her rented blue Honda sedan and was taking more pictures.

"Chandler holds a special place in my heart," Luke continued. "I hope that—" The ostrich's head snaked forward and Luke leaped back, but not before the bird got a beakful of roses. He began placidly chewing, the red petals sticking out of the side of his beak, his long-lashed eyelids drifting half-closed.

Luke looked from the bird to his mangled bouquet. Then he smiled at the crowd. "I've always wondered what it was like to be deflowered by Dirk Kennedy."

Meg grimaced at the bad joke but the crowd loved it. Amid laughter and applause, Luke handed the leash back to Joe Randolph and glanced at Meg with a can-we-go-now look. She nodded, and with a wave Luke headed back toward the truck as the pep band struck up the school fight song again.

"How'd I do?" Luke asked as Meg drove the truck carefully past waving onlookers and headed for the Bannister farm.

"Just fine." She chose not to elaborate. Maybe he was used to a constant stream of praise, but she didn't plan to provide that.

A cavalcade of cars and the TV van followed. He glanced in the rearview mirror. "This is incredible."

"You're a big hit around here."

"To tell you the truth, once I'm over the embarrassment of it all, I'll probably think it's funny as hell. I've dreaded coming back. Apparently I've been worried about the wrong things."

The hint of vulnerability piqued her curiosity. "What were you worried about?"

"I was considered nothing but a two-bit punk when I left. I was afraid the people around here would make me feel that way again."

She digested the comment, which didn't quite square with her image of him as an arrogant egomaniac. "Not likely, judging from this cavalcade."

Luke glanced around at the string of cars, trucks and vans. "Your parents weren't in that crowd, were they?"

"No."

He settled back in the seat. "Didn't think they would be. They still live down the road from Clint?"

"Yes. But I don't think they see him much."

"Didn't think they would."

They passed the house where Meg had grown up, and Luke glanced at it. "Kept the place up nice, didn't they?"

"You know Dad. Fresh coat of paint every five years, whether the place needs it or not. And Mom has a personal vendetta against weeds."

"Yeah, I remember."

Meg recalled the last discussion she'd had with her mother and father on the subject of Luke Bannister coming to town. "Don't spend too much time with him," her mother had warned. "You know those Hollywood types."

Her father had been more direct. "If you want to be the chamber's next president you'll guard your reputation. You've got enough strikes against you being young and a woman. If people see you hanging all over somebody like Luke Bannister, you won't have a chance."

Meg had assured them she had no intention of "hanging all over" Luke Bannister and adding to his overblown idea of his own importance.

They reached the Bannister farm, which stood in stark contrast to the Hennessy place. Luke's mother had died when he was eleven and Clint was nine. Meg remembered that Luke had tried to keep up his mother's flower beds after her death but one night his father, in a drunken rage fueled by grief, had plowed them under. Luke had given up on beautifying.

The weathered house, surrounded by a spring crop of new weeds, had a covered porch that ran the length of the front and a swing suspended from the rafters. Clint Bannister levered his lanky frame out of the swing as they climbed out of the truck and walked toward him. While Luke had taken after their dark-haired father, Clint resembled their mother, with light brown hair and gray eyes. Meg had always thought Clint had been spared the beatings Luke got because Clint reminded Orville of his late wife.

Clint took a swig of his beer and tipped his straw cowboy hat back with his thumb. "Looks like some famous person has come to call."

"Yeah." Luke held out his hand. "How are you, Clint?"

"Okay." Clint kept his hand at his side.

The insult stunned Meg. She didn't want Luke's opinion of himself to be unduly inflated, but she wouldn't wish this sort of public rejection on anyone. From the corner of her eye Meg saw the photographer closing in.

Luke lowered his hand and his gaze became wary. "Hope you don't mind my bunking in with you for a few days."

"Matter of fact, I do."

Meg squeezed her eyes shut. Clint was denying Luke access to his own home?

Luke nodded and backed up a step. "I see."

"I got work to do," Clint said. "About time to plant the fields." The camera flashed. "See that?" Clint gestured toward the young woman. "People taking pictures, the whole town gawking. I won't be able to get a damn thing done with you staying here. I suggest you find someplace else."

"All right." Luke turned toward Meg. "Let's go."

She stood there stupified. "Where?"

"Chandler has hotels and motels. I'll stay in one."

"Uh, okay." She doubted it. The town was already packed with visitors. This promised to be the biggest festival yet, and all the hotels in the area had been booked for weeks. "Let me talk to the TV folks a minute. I know they wanted footage of you here at home."

As she walked toward the television van she worried that the carefully stitched fabric of the festival she'd planned was starting to unravel. She'd seen the look in Clint's eyes. It was a familiar Bannister expression—she knew there was no point in arguing. There would only be a scene, and she didn't want news of a family feud showing up in some tabloid and besmirching the festival's good name.

She explained to the television crew that shots of the two brothers at home would be delayed. After repacking their equipment in the van, the crew drove away. The townspeople, too, turned their cars back down the road. Only the young photographer remained.

Clint went into the house and Luke headed for the truck. Meg followed him and climbed in behind the wheel. "We'll find a pay phone and make some calls."

His jaw tightened. "Right."

Forty minutes later, Meg had confirmed what she'd suspected earlier. Not a room anywhere. Even her parents weren't a possibility after what they'd said about Luke. And all her friends had out-of-town guests here for the festival. It was some sort of a record population swell, she knew, a record she should be proud of because her efforts had helped create this situation. It looked as if there was only one logical place for Luke to sleep that night. And it was not a very appropriate solution.

"Come on," she said, starting the truck. "We're going to my house."

"Sounds like a last resort."

She glanced at him as the truck idled in neutral. "Somebody might want to make something out of it. I'm in line to be the chamber's next president, and I'd rather not start any gossip."

"Chamber of commerce? Don't you have to own a business or something to be in that?"

"Dan and Chuck were partners in a computer consulting firm. I'm still part owner, and I help with bookkeeping. Since I want to go into politics, it's a perfect setup for me."

"So your mother was right."

"What do you mean?"

His gaze was steady. "I guess she didn't mention my call."

"What call? When?"

He shrugged and turned away. "It doesn't matter."

"Luke Bannister, stop that!" She felt an ancient frustration stirring her blood. He'd pulled a protective cloak around himself, just as he used to do when he was eighteen. At sixteen she'd never mustered the courage to challenge him when he shut her out. "Tell me about the call," she said.

As he stared silently out the window, she thought he wasn't going to answer her. Finally he said, "When I got the role in *Connections* I . . . wanted to tell you. I didn't really expect you to be home, but . . ." He shrugged again.

Her pulse quickened. So he had tried to contact her again. She made some mental calculations. "I must have been away at graduate school."

"Yeah. Political science major, your mother said. You and your fiancé were moving back to Chandler after graduation so you could get into local politics."

Her heart twisted. Of course her mother would have mentioned Dan, to underline that Meg was spoken for.

And her mother would have also conveniently forgotten to tell Meg about Luke's call. Meg wondered if her life would be different today if Luke had called when she was home on break. "Did you leave a number or anything?"

"Yeah. When you didn't call back, I figured . . . well, I could understand."

"I never got the message."

Slowly his gaze swung to hers. "And if you had?"

"I . . . I don't know."

He took a deep breath and let it out. "Look, let's find another place for me to stay. I don't want to be responsible for ending a promising political career."

"That's noble of you, but there is no other place. You're our guest of honor, Luke. I can't have you sleeping on a park bench, and I happen to have a spare room."

Luke angled his head toward the blue Honda still parked and waiting. "Then if you don't want gossip, I think you'd better ditch her before you take me home with you."

Meg glanced at the car and swore under her breath.

"You still got three hundred and fifty-two horses under this hood?" Luke asked.

"Yes. But if you blow my engine . . ."

"I won't. Trade places with me. If I could outrun Chandler's finest, I sure as hell can take that Honda."

3

MEG TRADED PLACES reluctantly, mentally calculating her options. Keeping Luke's visit impersonal was getting tougher by the minute. The knowledge that he'd tried to reach her before she'd married Dan had shaken her. He'd called after a triumph in his life. He wouldn't have done that without plans to reestablish contact between them. What would she have done if he'd wanted to see her again, if he'd invited her to L.A.?

Luke peeled away from the phone booth in a shower of gravel, throwing her against her seat belt. She grabbed the door handle with one hand and the edge of the seat with the other. "Watch for cops," he commanded, and sped around a corner. "And that damned blue Honda, of course. Where do you live?"

She told him.

"Okay. We'll take the long way home."

A fresh set of memories assaulted her. That had been their code phrase in high school when they'd decided to park. Luke would say softly, "Let's take the long way home tonight," and her heartbeat would thunder in her ears because she knew she'd soon be in his arms. She wondered if he remembered that's what he used to say. Probably not. He was a Hollywood star now, and he'd had torrid encounters by the dozen.

She checked for police cars as Luke veered off onto a side street. The blue Honda followed them. "Still back there," she said.

"I'll lose her." He passed a sedan and stepped down hard on the gas. "Kermit still has what it takes."

Wind from the open window buffeted Meg's face and tangled her hair. She glanced over at Luke. "I don't think you ever drove like this when I was around."

"Nope." He kept his eyes on the road. The wind had tousled his dark hair, making him look more like the renegade she'd known in high school.

Meg battled her volatile emotions. Watching Luke court danger inspired a feeling that she'd never had with anyone else. He'd always been able to make her feel this way—wild and ready to take risks. She'd almost forgotten the sensation. At sixteen her yearnings had been vague but powerful. They were still powerful . . . and no longer vague.

"See the Honda?"

Meg checked in the rearview mirror. "Nope."

"Keep watching. I'll slip down a few more side streets before we head for your house. Good thing she doesn't know the town. It's amazing I can still find my way around, the way things have changed. But the basic grid's still the same." The tires screeched as he rounded another curve.

"I'll probably hear about this tomorrow. Everybody recognizes this truck."

"Tell them I was practicing for a new episode of *Connections*."

"Do you usually use your celebrity status to get out of a jam?"

His eyes narrowed. "Only when it gets me into one."

CLINT STAYED INSIDE the house until the last car pulled away. Then he popped the top of another beer and returned to the porch swing. So his hotshot brother thought he could move in and take over the place after ten years. Probably envisioned some sappy homecoming scene like when Dolly Parton did her Christmas television special back in the hills of Tennessee. Hah.

Clint took a long swallow of his beer and thought about his brother—how Luke had made his bed ten years ago, taking off and leaving Clint to deal with their boozed-up old man and a neglected cotton farm. Luke probably thought he'd made up for that by deeding over his share of the farm to Clint when the old man died. Clint didn't think so. He'd trade his life around here for a cushy job like Luke's in a minute.

The next few days would be sickening, with everybody gushing over Luke, the TV star. Once upon a time Clint thought Luke was pretty special, too. Then Luke cut out for fun in the sun, and before too long somebody came offering Luke a job making commercials. The old man had been so friggin' proud of that it had made Clint want to throw up. He never appreciated Clint's working in the fields until he was tanned darker than the foreman, Juan Soledad. Just kept carrying on about Luke in some stupid jock-itch commercial.

Then, when the old man died, Luke couldn't even be bothered to come home for the funeral. So Clint got the farm. Big deal. He gazed out at the weed-choked front yard and across the plowed fields to his right. In point of fact he had a little spare time right now. He planned to hold off another week before planting, let the ground dry out a little more. But he didn't want to spend that week with his older brother.

Down the road he saw a car approaching from town, a blue sedan. When it turned into the drive he thought about going inside and not answering the door, but he hated the thought of being chased from his own front porch while he was enjoying a beer.

The person who got out looked familiar. Where had he seen somebody wearing a Dodgers baseball cap on backward? Oh, yeah. That crazy fan who had stayed behind to take pictures. She had sunglasses on now, and no cameras strapped around her body. She had a decent figure, although she obviously didn't much care if anybody noticed. Her tank top and baggy shorts looked as if they belonged to somebody three sizes larger. Spiky sections of her brown hair stuck out from her baseball cap. She was chewing gum.

"He's not here," Clint said as she approached the porch. "So if you're looking for a scoop, you'll have to go someplace else."

She shoved her hands into her pockets and braced her legs. "You could just be saying that." Pop went the gum.

"I could be, but I'm not."

"I lost him on the back roads. There was always the chance you two staged that little disagreement and he doubled back here."

"Didn't happen."

She hesitated and chewed her gum as if weighing the possibilities.

"Hell, go on and look through the house if you don't believe me. I don't want you lurking in the bushes all night hoping he'll show up. I might accidentally shoot you or something." She stiffened, and he smiled. So she wasn't quite as tough as she tried to look. He took a swig of his beer. "How old are you?"

"Never mind that."

"You're supposed to say old enough, and stick out your chin. If you're going to look like some kind of mean kid, you'll have to learn to talk back like one."

Her shoulders slumped a little and she started to turn around.

"Want a beer?" She glanced back at him. "I'm going to assume you're old enough to drink." She nodded. "Then come on and have a seat." He got out of the swing and went in for another can. He had no idea why he was doing this, except he was a sucker for people when they were down and out, when everything they tried seemed to blow up in their faces. She looked that way.

When he returned she was sitting on the porch steps. He handed her the beer, and she popped the top with a murmured thanks. After sticking her wad of gum on the edge of the can, she practically chugalugged the whole thing. When she came up for air, she gave him a tentative smile. "Thanks. I was so excited I didn't eat or drink anything on the plane. After that there was no time."

Clint leaned against the porch railing and sipped his beer. "You got a name?"

"Ansel Wiggins. I was named after Ansel Adams, the photographer."

"And you're following in his footsteps?"

She laughed. "Hardly. He was an artist. I just chase celebrities and try to make a buck."

"You like it?"

"Yeah." Her face became more animated. "It's like a game, trying to figure out how to trap them when they least expect it. In L.A. I'm pretty good at that, but out here I don't know the territory."

"How long have you been doing this?"

She ducked her head and mumbled something.

"What?"

"Six months, okay? I'm new. I haven't actually sold any pictures yet, but I got a lead that Luke Bannister might have a motion picture contract coming up, and the part sounds decent. It could make him a superstar, and if I get some hot shots of him, I'll make a bundle."

Clint stared down the road. "I don't understand why he tried to ditch you, then. I thought the whole idea was to get his damned picture in the papers."

"Not *my* kind of pictures. His agent only wants the publicity photos his office releases. Mine aren't always so flattering."

"Ah."

"How come you didn't want Luke staying here?"

He glanced down at her. Nice skin. And she wasn't as naive as he might have thought, either. That wasn't an idle question. "No comment."

"Does he visit here much?"

"Look, Ansel, I may be a farm boy, but I'm not stupid. Back off."

"I never thought you were stupid." She stood up and stretched. He noticed the nice muscle definition in her calves. Then she handed him the beer can. "You recycle these?"

He didn't, but he took it, anyway. He should start, just like he should mow the weeds in the front yard and get the house painted. When Luke had arrived today, Clint had seen the place through Luke's eyes and hadn't much liked the view. Damn Luke for coming back and stirring things up.

"Thanks for the beer," Ansel said. "Guess I'll go buy a map and learn the country before I start the chase again."

For one crazy moment he thought about helping her. It would be kind of fun, and it would have the added benefit of irritating the hell out of Luke. But no, there were some things even he wouldn't stoop to. "Good hunting," he called after her as she walked back to her rental car.

"Don't worry. I'll leave here with something good."

He wondered if she'd succeed. It would serve his brother right.

LUKE PULLED INTO the gravel drive of the house Meg directed him to and parked behind a silver BMW. When Meg didn't say anything about having company, he reasoned that the silver car was hers. Yet she'd brought the old truck to the airport. He liked her spunk. "Wasn't this the Whitley place?"

"They sold out and moved to Oregon. Dan and I contacted the developer before he tore the house down, but we couldn't afford to buy all the land, too. Since we didn't want to farm, the developer subdivided the rest."

He turned off the motor. "It's a nice house."

"Thanks."

And not so different from the one Clint had booted him out of this afternoon, he thought, climbing out of the truck. Except that this one was in good repair. Maybe he should have guessed Clint would turn him away, but he hadn't thought Clint was bitter enough to deny him a roof over his head. Tomorrow he'd have to go over and straighten things out with his little brother.

For tonight, though, he'd have the bittersweet experience of sleeping in Meg's house, the one she'd once shared with her husband. How many times in the past ten years had he tried to imagine the house she lived in? Too many to count. He glanced at the frame construction, double-hung windows and front porch. A couple of pink geranium plants sat in pots on either side of the screen door. The yard was neat, but not fussy, with a mulberry tree for shade. It was a family kind of house. Meg had probably planned to hang a swing from the tree, like the one he remembered at the back of her house twenty years ago.

He heard the clang of the tailgate and turned to find Meg wrestling his stuff out of the truck bed. "Here, I'll do that."

"I just thought we'd better go inside before the woman in the blue Honda gets lucky and drives past here. In fact, why don't I take this inside while you pull the truck around behind the house? I'll let you in through the kitchen."

He grinned. "So this is going to be a backdoor affair?" When her eyes narrowed and her cheeks turned pink, he regretted his impulsive wisecrack. "Sorry. I'll move the truck."

As he drove around the side of the house he cursed himself for making the remark. It had been a bad joke, implying all the wrong things—that he found the idea of a secret affair with her intriguing and wouldn't want anything more solid than that.

He parked the truck in front of a battered garage that looked as if it hadn't been used since the Whitleys moved away. As he got out of the truck a golden retriever bounded toward him. He scratched the dog's ears. Of course she'd have a dog, a big fluffy one like this. Glancing up, he saw Meg standing in the open kitchen doorway smiling at him, her corn-silk hair loose around her shoulders the way he'd always loved it best. His heart turned over. Backdoor affair, indeed. He wanted the same thing he'd dreamed about since he was six years old—to marry Meg Hennessy.

THE MINUTE HE STEPPED into her house, Meg knew she'd been unwise to think this would work. But she could come up with nothing else on such short notice. Maybe tomorrow she could find him a room. She'd have to—

he was too powerful a force to deal with at such close range. "I see you've met Dog-breath."

"Yep." He let the dog inside and closed the kitchen door with a soft click. "I'm really sorry about what I said a minute ago."

"Don't be silly. It was just a joke." Meg opened up a cabinet and scooped out some dry food for Dog-breath. She poured it into his bowl and spilled some in the process. He started munching noisily as she bent down to retrieve the stray pieces. Her hands were shaking.

"Bad joke. Here, let me help." He crouched down next to her.

She waved him away."I've got it." Her heart pounded as if she'd been running. "Let me show you your room. You can pick up your things on the way through the living room. I left them on the couch."

"Okay."

She led him through the house and took several steadying breaths as she walked. Maybe having him here would get easier once her nervousness wore off. After all, they'd known each other since they were children. She paused before the guest bedroom with its brass double bed. "Here you are. The bath is across the hall. After I put some sheets on the bed you'll be all set."

He walked into the room and laid his garment bag and duffel on the fringed white spread. "Isn't this the same bed you had in your room when we were kids?"

"Same headboard and footboard, different mattress. You have quite a memory."

"For some things. Listen, if you'll go get the sheets, I'll make the bed myself. I don't want you to go to any extra trouble."

"It's no trouble." But making up his bed might be far too erotic for her strained nervous system.

"Come on, Meg. Get the darned sheets. We'll do it together."

Protesting again would make more of it than was already there. She retreated to the linen closet and returned with a set of blue-and-white striped sheets. He'd already hung his garment bag in the closet and put his duffel on the closet floor. He stripped back the spread and draped it over a pine rocker in the corner. Then he walked to the other side of the bed and held out his hand. "Throw me a corner."

She did, and they began making the bed as if they'd been doing it together for years. Except Meg couldn't shake off the feeling they were assembling the equivalent of a nuclear bomb. "The sheets smell great. I bet you hung them on the line."

"I did." She'd forgotten the high level of Luke's sensory awareness. When they were dating, he'd made her try out at least twenty perfumes in the drugstore and finally decided he liked her natural scent best. She'd never worn perfume after that, although that had been really stupid, she thought now. He'd had way too much influence on her life.

"I haven't slept on sun-dried sheets since I left Arizona." He tucked in the top sheet and reached for the bedspread. As he handed a section of it to Meg, their eyes met. "It's great of you to let me stay here," he said in a low voice. "I won't abuse the privilege."

She dropped the section of bedspread as if it were on fire. "You certainly won't!" His announcement sounded as if it were all up to him!

He chuckled and shook his head. "Right. Toss me a pillowcase, Meg."

She did, and wondered how the act of catching a pillowcase in midair could be so sensuous. Or why she was so fascinated with watching him tuck the pillow under his chin and work the case up one end of the pillow. He shook the pillow into place and plumped it before laying it on the bed. Meg followed suit and set hers beside it. So inviting, those two pillows. An unwanted ache settled between her thighs, an ache she hadn't felt in a long time. She busied herself smoothing the spread and adjusting the fringe. She could never acknowledge her attraction to him, mainly because he seemed to expect she would be attracted, the egotistical lout.

"I think the network said something about a dinner tonight."

She looked up in dismay, belatedly remembering the scheduled affair. "You're right." She glanced at her watch. "We have exactly an hour before we have to be out of here. I told them we'd be at the San Marcos for cocktails by five-thirty, and I haven't even checked my messages yet."

"Then you'd better get going. Don't let me interfere with what you have to do in the next few days."

She gazed across the bed at him. He was doing it again, assuming his presence would unsettle and distract her. He must be used to having that effect on women. She'd be damned if she'd let him know he bothered her at all. "I won't let you interfere." She spun on her heel and nearly walked into the wall. Correcting course, she managed to make it through the door without tripping. She didn't look back, afraid she'd discover him laughing at her. "See you in an hour."

She hurried down the hall to her office. The message light was blinking on her answering machine. One of the exhibitors wanted their booth placement changed to a corner space, and someone wanted to know if they could still get a raffle ticket for a date with Luke Bannister. The last message was from Didi, who hoped Meg had been able to find Luke a place to stay.

"I found him one all right," Meg muttered to herself as she walked into her bedroom and closed the door. "Let's hope it's not my downfall."

As she showered and dressed for dinner, she replayed every moment of being with Luke since he'd arrived. No question that he had her blood racing as it hadn't in years. Even the mundane job of making a bed took on new significance when Luke was around.

She hadn't been in a bedroom with him since they were nine and eleven years old. That was the time Clint had had the flu and had to stay home. She and Luke had been playing Parcheesi in her room, but had become bored with it. After they'd goofed around some, Luke had suggested kissing with tongues. He'd kissed her before, just lips, but this was different. She hadn't liked the tongue part at nine. At sixteen she'd liked it far too much.

As a nine-year-old with no secrets, she'd made the mistake of telling her mother about Luke putting his tongue in her mouth, and her mother had forbidden them to be alone again. She'd branded Luke as "too sexually advanced for his age."

Her mother's description hadn't meant much to Meg then, but when puberty hit she recalled with new interest that Luke was supposed to be "sexually advanced," and he became the focus of her erotic fantasies. When he finally asked her out during her sophomore year in high school, she thought she'd died and gone to heaven. Her parents had had a somewhat different reaction.

But they allowed her to go out with him as long as she kept strict curfews and double-dated. The dates always started out as a foursome, but sometime during the evening Meg and Luke would usually end up alone, a move probably engineered by Luke, she realized now.

During those precious moments alone with him, she learned that "sexually advanced" meant that he kissed like no other boy she'd ever known. His kisses softened parts of her and set others on fire. It was she who unbuttoned her blouse the first time, because her breasts ached for his touch, it was she who guided his hand beneath the elastic of her panties. She would have let him make love to her, and she knew he'd wanted to. But each night he'd gently close up her blouse with shaking fingers, kiss her softly on the mouth, and take her home still a virgin. She fell hopelessly in love.

Then came the day he'd swaggered up to her locker and told her he wouldn't be asking her out again. She was too young for him, he'd said, too inexperienced. He needed to date women his own age.

Meg still remembered the pain that had engulfed her for weeks. She'd lost fifteen pounds and almost failed geometry. Each time she'd seen Luke with one of the senior girls she'd wanted to scream. But eventually the hurt had turned to anger, and by the time Luke had left town, she'd sworn to everyone that she didn't care if a California earthquake swallowed him whole.

And now he was sleeping under her roof, this "sexually advanced" man of twenty-eight, who no longer was just her fantasy, but the fantasy of thousands of women. And if he could kiss that well at eighteen, what must he be like now? Meg shoved the thought away with a feeling of panic. She could not afford to find out.

4

LUKE BUTTONED a paisley vest over his white silk turtleneck and pulled on a gray jacket. He already missed his jeans and T-shirt, but his agent, who had supervised the packing for this trip, had reminded him about his image. The people at this dinner expected Hollywood glamour, so Luke would give it to them.

He smoothed his hair with his palms, pocketed his wallet and wandered out into Meg's living room to commune with her dog. He liked Dog-breath. Once he'd had a dog, a mutt, but his father had kicked it around so unmercifully that Luke had given it away to save its life.

Dog-breath clambered to his feet from his position on a rag rug in front of the green-and-white plaid couch. The dog was the perfect finishing touch to the country setting of the room. An antique pine cupboard, rattan chairs with dark green cushions and a brick fireplace still holding ashes from a recent fire gave Luke a picture that contrasted sharply with his sterile L.A. apartment decorated mostly in silver and gray.

Dog-breath pushed his damp muzzle against Luke's hand. Lowering himself to the couch, Luke rubbed the silky head and scratched down the dog's backbone until he wriggled with pleasure. When Luke leaned back against the cushions, Dog-breath put his head on Luke's knee for more attention.

"We all love to be petted, don't we, Dog-breath?" Luke thought about how long it had been since someone had touched him with honest affection. The simulated kind on the set didn't count. But even his real-life love affairs had been more about sex than love. Once he became well-known as Dirk Kennedy, he suspected his last two partners had imagined themselves going to bed with Dirk, not Luke. Heck, maybe they had. There was only one woman he'd trusted enough to be himself with, and she was just down the hall, dressing to go out to dinner with him.

But somebody had scripted this wrong. They'd given Meg political ambitions in a small town and stymied what might have been a wonderful weekend of rekindling an old flame. Cozying up to the parade grand marshal while she was supposed to be running the festival wouldn't do much for her image. He could be a real liability to her future if he acted on his impulses this weekend. And beyond this weekend, what did he have to offer? He was tied to L.A., and he couldn't ask her to give up everything she'd worked for in exchange for a life-style she'd probably hate. Had he found her again, only to be forced to give her up, just as he had ten years ago?

Then she came down the hall and he felt as if someone had punched him in the gut. He was no longer an unsophisticated farm boy. He'd escorted women who shopped on Rodeo Drive, beautiful women whose entire lives revolved around dressing well. Yet when Meg appeared, he rose from the couch in homage.

"It's okay?" Her prickly behavior had given way to feminine uncertainty about her appearance.

Maybe his own flashy outfit had prompted her insecurity, he thought, but whatever had, her tentative question tugged at his heartstrings. "Yeah," he said softly. "More than okay." The dress was the color of new leaves, and had the delicate look of fresh growth. Sleeveless, it crossed over her breasts and stayed in place somehow without buttons, reminding him of the robes of a Greek goddess. A wide belt the same color green emphasized her waist and the swell of her hips beneath the gently flowing skirt. She'd piled her hair on top of her head in a way he'd never seen, exposing her tender nape and the curve of her earlobes. Pearls dangled from her ears and circled her throat.

"You're sure?" She peered at him, as if his scrutiny made her doubt her choice. "You can tell me the truth."

"You wouldn't believe me if I told you the truth."

"Yes, I would. You've been out in the world more than I have, so I trust your judgment. If there's something wrong with this, I can change."

She really didn't know the effect she had on him. His arms ached to hold her. "The truth is, you are the most beautiful woman I've ever seen."

She blushed and looked away. "Now *that's* ridiculous. I'm no fool, Luke. I'll get my coat and we can go."

He followed her as she walked to the living room closet and pulled out a soft beige coat. "I said you wouldn't believe me."

"You're right. I don't." She sounded angry again, as if she suspected his motives for complimenting her. "I watch the Academy Awards, too, you know. I know what movie stars look like."

"So do I." He took the coat and held it for her. "You've got them beat."

"Luke, don't try to flatter me. Please."

He couldn't win, so he said nothing while nestling the coat over her shoulders. He breathed deep, savoring the scent of her clean, fresh skin, and for a moment he gripped her shoulders and longed to nuzzle the spot where a tendril of hair had escaped to curl across her nape. Then he released her.

He never remembered curbing an urge like that before. He'd never had to. In many ways his life had been tough, and he'd taken his share of knocks, but when it came to women, he'd always found a welcome smile, eager arms. But here with Meg, he feared rejection for the first time.

MEG LET OUT HER BREATH as Luke moved away from her. The moment he'd taken her coat, she'd wanted to snatch it back. But that would have looked stupid, as if she weren't lady enough to accept a man's gesture of helping her on with her coat. The problem was that the action brought him so close she could smell the mint of his shaving cream and feel his breath on her neck. When he briefly gripped her shoulders after putting on the coat, her knees grew weak.

She half feared he might turn her around and kiss her. Then she remembered why. That had been a little ritual from their dating days. When they left a dance or a movie, he'd help her on with her coat, turn her around and give her a soft kiss, as if his lips would protect her from the cold as much as her coat would. Back then, she believed they had.

"We'll take the BMW," she said, pulling out a small evening bag from the coat closet. She transferred keys and wallet from her shoulder bag hanging just inside the closet door. "That way maybe your friend in the Honda won't find you right away."

Luke followed her out the front door. "We'll probably be free of her until opening ceremonies tomorrow. After that she won't let me out of her sight."

A cool breeze ruffled the tendrils that had escaped from Meg's upswept hair. She slipped on her sunglasses to protect against the glare of a sun that wouldn't set for another hour. "Dodging people like that sounds like a grim way to live."

He put on his pair of designer sunglasses. "For her or me?"

"Both of you, actually." As she unlocked the passenger side of the BMW, she glanced at him. With his paisley vest, his dark hair combed into place and sunglasses concealing his blue eyes, he looked like a movie star. The emotional distance between them seemed to increase each time she was reminded that he no longer lived in her world. She slid into the driver's seat and started the car.

"I guess I take this paparazzi thing in stride because I'm used to being watched."

She glanced at him. "Oh, really?"

"Yeah. So are you."

"No, I'm not, and I wouldn't like—"

"Then why do we have to worry about me staying at your house? What's all this about guarding your reputation so you can move into the political scene?"

She fell silent. He had a point. She didn't have a photographer following her, but she might as well have. Chandler folks took lots of mental pictures and reproduced them on cue to interested parties. It was the small-town way of keeping track of everyone, a habit that continued despite Chandler's growing size.

"You're no more free than I am, Meg."

"You're right."

"For the heck of it, let's pretend that we could do anything we wanted right now. What would you do?"

"I...I don't know." And she didn't dare let her imagination work on the idea, either.

"I know what I'd do. I'd get in the truck, drive out to the desert, build a fire, roast hot dogs and drink beer."

"Hmm."

"Then I'd turn on the truck radio to KNIX and dance."

She arched a brow. "By yourself?"

"Not if I could convince you to come along."

As her heartbeat speeded up, Meg remembered Didi's warning. Apparently the time had come to take some defensive action. She took a long, shaky breath. "Okay, we need to get something straight. Neither of us is a teenager anymore." Her heartbeat pounded in her ears, but she pushed on. "You're a rising star in Hollywood and I have my eye on a political career in

Arizona. If I stay in Chandler and keep my nose clean, I have a good chance of being in the state legislature one day. And I don't plan to stop there. I want to run for Congress eventually."

He grinned. "And the White House?"

"Go ahead and laugh, but you never know. I might, if everything falls into place for me."

"I'm not laughing. I think you'd be great. You've always had the ability to inspire people."

"And you're a natural on screen. I think we've both found what we were meant to do and we can go as high as we choose. We . . . shouldn't let some pleasant memories get us off track."

"Nice speech. You'll make a good politician."

She glanced at him and saw his smile. "Luke, I'm only trying to—"

"I know." His expression became serious. "And I understand what you're trying to say."

"I hope so."

"Believe it or not, I came to the same conclusion not long ago."

"Good." Her sigh contained both relief and disappointment.

"Are we telling anyone where I'm staying?"

She hesitated. "I hate lying, but the fewer people who know about it the better."

"Then leave it to me. Don't forget that I act for a living."

I won't, she thought. It was a good thing he'd reminded her. Maybe all his apparent interest in her, which she'd felt honor-bound to turn aside, had been an act. Luke Bannister had been put on this earth to charm women, and he did so effortlessly, without thinking. What she interpreted as interest might simply be his normal behavior with any woman.

Embarrassment heated her cheeks. She might have just made a colossal fool of herself with her prim little speech. Luke probably had no intentions toward her except those he had toward any woman: to bring her under his spell for the time he was with her. After that, she'd be forgotten as he wove his magic for the next willing victim.

THROUGHOUT DINNER in the San Marcos's Nineteen-Twelve restaurant, named for the year the hotel was built, Meg watched Luke in action. As a boy he had once scrambled under barbed-wire fences with her. Now the man looked perfectly at ease in the subdued atmosphere of the candlelit room, where guests nestled into cushioned rattan chairs and dined from gold-rimmed plates.

Luke entertained the large table of city council members and festival organizers with insider stories about the entertainment industry. He took their teasing about his steamy character with good-natured laughter. His performance was flawless, and Meg was sure that a performance was exactly what he was giving.

Back when they were dating, Luke had taken her out for a special dinner at Serranos, a cozy Mexican restaurant that still reminded Meg of Luke every time she went in. He'd been much quieter in those days, much less sure of himself. But she still remembered the way he'd gazed at her across the table, the candle flame dancing in his eyes, as if he were memorizing how she looked. Her little speech tonight notwithstanding, she caught him gazing at her that way again. Her hand shook as she reached for her water goblet and took a long, calming drink.

Over dessert, Didi asked about Clint, and Luke chuckled as he described his little brother's understandable behavior. Meg would have bet good money that Clint's rejection had hurt Luke, but no one would ever know it to see him brush the incident aside now. True to his word, he explained that he and Meg had worked out a place for him to stay, but they weren't going to reveal the location because Luke preferred not to have the press camped outside his door. The story wasn't even a lie, Meg thought in admiration. Luke wouldn't make such a bad politician himself.

The talk turned to last-minute festival preparations, and Meg felt Luke's gaze rest on her as she handled the questions and problems. No doubt about it, she liked being in charge and leaving her fingerprints on various enterprises. She enjoyed a certain amount of the limelight.

By nine o'clock napkins were laid beside plates and chairs moved back. There were handshakes and last parting jokes all around. Didi edged over to Meg and murmured under the flow of goodbyes, "See? This will be great, having him here for the festival."

"He does seem to be a good choice."

"People will remember the success of the event for a long time, and that's good PR for you."

Meg nodded. "By the way, nice outfit." Didi tended toward plumpness, but she knew how to dress in flowing material and brilliant colors that accentuated her dark hair and eyes, so people seldom noticed her extra weight.

Didi smiled, showing her dimples. "Thanks. You look great, too. And what was all that double-talk about where Luke's staying? Who's the paranoid person who's putting him up?"

Meg gazed at her meaningfully without answering.

"Uh-oh."

"It was that or a bench in the park."

"Well, be careful, sweetie. He's a charmer."

Meg glanced across the table. Luke was standing there, his head bent forward as he listened to something Mayor Garvey was saying to him. Then he smiled and winked at the mayor's wife. "That he is," she murmured.

As they walked out through the hotel lobby to the hotel entrance and the valet-parking stand, Meg silently rehearsed her excuses for turning in early. She didn't dare sit around making small talk with Luke after they got home.

Once they were in the car and driving down the road he leaned back against the headrest. "Well, that's over."

"You sound glad."

"I am."

"You looked as if you were having a ball."

"Never let them see you sweat."

"You were nervous? Come on."

"Some of those people wanted my head on a pole when I was back in high school. I was waiting for somebody to bring up the old days."

"So you kept them rolling in the aisles with Hollywood stories, so they wouldn't have time."

"Something like that."

"Well, I can testify from personal experience now. You're a terrific actor."

"And you're a born organizer. I was impressed, Meg."

She laughed. "Quite a mutual admiration society we have here." She wished she had some of his acting skills right now. She wanted to feign exhaustion but she was strung tighter than a guitar string.

"Let's not go straight back," he said.

Good. A distraction. "Where do you want to go?"

"I'd like to see the high school again, for one thing. If we take a tour at night, I can get away with it. By tomorrow I won't be able to do that in peace."

"Okay. The high school it is." She turned back toward town and headed down Arizona Avenue. "The main building is the same, but a lot's been added on since you left. The Chandler Center for the Arts was built right next to the school, so the city and the school district have joint use. It's an amazing performance center, Luke."

"I can see I chose the right tour guide."

She bridled at his indulgent tone. "Maybe it's not Hollywood, but I think even you will be impressed.

Chandler has an exciting future, whether you realize it or not. We project growth in the next ten years of—"

"There's that chip on your shoulder again."

"Well, your comment sounded like a patronizing pat on the head."

"If it did, I'm sorry. I just get a kick out of your chamber of commerce plugs. It takes me right back to high school, when you were running for president of the sophomore class and making speeches about school pride. You were so . . . so—"

"Cute?" Meg smacked the steering wheel. "Don't you dare call me that."

"Well, if it makes you feel any better, you're not cute anymore."

"Good!"

"The fact is, you're damned beautiful."

She almost missed the turn down the side street where she'd planned to park the car. As she veered into it, the tires squealed. "I thought we could get out and walk." She turned off the motor and headlights in a flash and whipped out of the car. Once on the pavement she took a deep breath of the cool night air. Twice in one night he'd called her beautiful. It was enough to turn a girl's head. But she wasn't a girl anymore, and her head must stay firmly facing in the direction of her goals.

As they started down the sidewalk together, she shoved her hands into her coat pockets. Her heels made a hollow click, click, click on the concrete as they approached the Center for the Arts. The rhythm of her steps mingled with the splash of water as they neared the fountain in front of the building's curved facade. Soaring glass panels revealed sparkling chandeliers illuminating the lobby.

Luke paused to gaze up at the building. "First class, Meg."

"You should see the performance area. Red velvet seats, and sections revolve to face different stages. We can have three events going on at once in there."

"I remember playing on that old high school stage."

"I remember you staggering on that old high school stage."

"Drunk was the only way I could handle being there. I had the worst case of stage fright you can imagine."

Meg stared at him in surprise. Luke had won the lead in the school musical after he'd broken up with her. At that point, she'd no longer been privy to his thoughts. He'd had a fling with his co-star and Meg hadn't been able to like her ever since. "I never guessed that you were scared."

"Fortunately the booze wore off before the thing was over, and I had a chance to find out you can hide behind your character when you're acting. If I hadn't discovered that, I'd probably still be a California beach bum waiting tables by night and surfing by day."

"You actually planned to get into acting when you went to L.A.?"

"It was in the back of my mind, but I didn't know the first thing about breaking in. Then the second luckiest thing in my life happened. One of my surfing buddies heard about a job doing a commercial. He had some contacts, got us a test, and I landed the role."

"Selling what?"

"Stuff for jock itch."

Meg laughed in spite of herself. "And then?"

"The third luckiest thing in my life. One of the writers for *Connections* saw the commercial and I fitted his image of a character he was creating."

"Dirk Kennedy."

"Yeah."

"You said those were the second and third luckiest things to happen in your life. What was the first?"

He hesitated and glanced down at her. "Growing up on a farm next to yours."

She had to ask. His statement had been made with a simplicity that convinced her it wasn't a line. Their childhood memories meant as much to him as they had to her. Her resolve to keep her distance slipped down another notch.

He angled his head toward the historic old high school farther down the block. "Let's keep walking."

A soft breeze carried the scent of freshly cut grass to Meg as she matched her stride to Luke's. Her arm brushed his and she mumbled an apology while clenching her hands in her pockets to keep from reaching out to him. Above them, palm fronds waved in the night sky, and aleppo pines stood sentinel on either side of the main entrance to the school.

"It hasn't changed," Luke said, facing the two-story tan building with its massive Greek columns and broad front steps. "Still looks like a Norman Rockwell version of what a high school should be."

"I guess you weren't very happy here."

"No, but I brought a lot of my problems on myself. If I ever had a kid, I'd like him to go to a school like this."

"It's a long commute from L.A."

"Yeah." He laughed dryly. "You have a point."

She could sense the tug-of-war in him, good memories fighting bad. But even if the good memories won, he'd already made his life elsewhere. She might have been important in his life once, but he'd moved beyond her reach. "Want to see the rest?"

"Sure. Is the oak tree still around back?"

"Still there."

"I'd like to see that."

Meg led the way around the side of the building to the back courtyard, where the gnarled oak grew. Security lights brightened the grounds, except for a shadowed area beneath the oak's dark branches. Luke walked over and propped one foot on the brick planter box surrounding the tree. "I spent some good times here, waiting by this tree."

Meg moved into the shadows with him. "Me, too," she answered truthfully. The tree had been their meeting place between classes and at lunch. Every day, she'd raced to get to that tree, but somehow he'd always arrived ahead of her. She could still see him lounging there wearing opaque sunglasses, jeans and a white T-shirt with the sleeves rolled, his books carelessly tossed at his feet. He'd be talking with one of his buddies, but the minute she arrived, he'd turn all his attention on her.

School officials and local police might have considered Luke a menace to the community, but every girl at Chandler High had a crush on him. Because he'd chosen Meg, she'd felt like royalty. Ten years later he was making her feel that way again, acting as if he hadn't dumped her unceremoniously all those years ago. It was almost as if she'd been the one to discard him.

She gazed up through the tree branches and saw a glowing half moon that made her think of a quarter stuck in a jukebox. Her and Luke's song had turned out to be so heartbreakingly appropriate—Willie Nelson's "You Were Always on My Mind," a song about a neglected love affair.

Meg swallowed the lump in her throat. Maybe she was asking to be hurt again, but she had to know. "What happened, Luke? Back then."

He pushed away from the planter box and walked toward her. "I was asked not to talk about it, and I promised I wouldn't. But things look a little different to me now. I decided before I came to Chandler that if you asked me, I'd break that promise."

Her heart thudded in her chest. "About what? Who made you promise?"

"Your father."

She had a sick feeling she wasn't going to like what he was about to say, but she'd brought up the painful subject and couldn't back away now. "Tell me."

"It seems he got a report that we'd been seen out parking. Several times."

Heat coursed through her veins. Once she would have been thoroughly embarrassed by that knowledge, but now all she could think of was the passion of those nights.

"He got me alone one afternoon when he knew you weren't around. I think you had to work on the posters for your election campaign or something. He explained how different you and I were, how you were going to be somebody someday, and I obviously wasn't. He was giving me a clear message to stay away from you."

"You broke up with me because my father told you to?" The Luke she'd known would have stormed away from such a lecture.

"Not exactly. I knew your parents didn't like me. His opinion wasn't hot news. But he had an extra little persuader. He'd seen Clint coming out of the back of old man Baker's hardware store late one night, his arms full of merchandise. That was before Baker put in the alarm system. You know the trouble Clint was in. One more arrest and he'd have been locked up. I promised to straighten Clint out...and break up with you...if your father wouldn't tell what he saw."

She stood there, her head reeling. "My father *blackmailed* you?"

"I guess that's one way of putting it. Looking back on it, I don't much blame him. I wasn't any good for you, but I was too selfish to see that at the time."

"But he meddled in my life, in both our lives!"

"Parents figure they have a right to do that sometimes, especially if they think their kid is in danger."

"I can't believe he did that to me. As if I had no sense. I wasn't in danger. I was—"

"You were in danger," Luke countered softly.

At his tone, the memories pushed away her anger—and she acknowledged that in the splendor of his arms she would have denied him nothing.

"I tell myself I wouldn't have lost my head with you, but who knows? And even if we'd used protection, nothing's foolproof. Your father's nightmare was that his beautiful, intelligent sixteen-year-old daughter would come to him and confess the town punk had made her pregnant."

She stared at him, her heart pounding, her whole body at flash point. His confession had changed everything. If he touched her now, all her repressed longings would burst into flame.

He sighed and ran his fingers through his hair, mussing the careful styling job and making him look more like the boy she used to know. "I feel as if we're right back where we started."

She swallowed, unable to speak.

"Here you are, working toward a career in politics, and here I am, the potential scandal-maker who could ruin your chances. I'm only here for the weekend. We both know I'm not right for you, any more than I was ten years ago." He looked straight at her and lowered his voice to a murmur. "But you see, I still want you, Meg."

His words flowed over her like hot lava. A familiar ache began deep within her and spread quickly. This feeling hadn't been the product of teenage hormones ten years ago, as she'd tried to rationalize since then. The catalyst had been Luke.

"The trouble is, I'm not as selfish as I was at eighteen. I'm no longer willing to risk your reputation to get what I want. If your father showed up and told me you didn't need some Hollywood type screwing up your life for a weekend of fun, I'd have to agree with him."

She stepped closer, drawn to him as if pulled by an invisible tether. "Is that what you are? Some Hollywood type?"

"Yes." He took a deep breath and gazed down at her. "I love the excitement, the challenge of fighting for the spotlight. I won't kid you about that. I'm hooked on this star thing, which means I'd never settle down in Chandler. You need a tractor salesman, a cotton farmer, somebody who'd be there for you."

The urge to touch him became irresistible. She slid her fingers up the silk of his paisley vest and felt the rapid beating of his heart. "I've been watching *Connections.* You're a natural on screen." His arms crept beneath her open coat and around her waist, cradling her gently. At the contact, she trembled and looked up into his face.

His half smile was barely visible in the dim light. "I thought you weren't a fan of the show."

"I decided to watch it recently, to familiarize myself with the characters in case the media asked me—"

"Save the speeches for the voters, Hennessy." He started rubbing her back with light, teasing strokes.

It took so little for him to arouse her. She was almost angry with him for doing it so easily. "What do you want me to say? That I never miss an episode, that I'm driven to watch you day after day?"

"Are you?"

Somehow her arms were around his neck and she was on tiptoe. Her mouth hovered inches from his. "Now I am. Are you satisfied?"

His embrace tightened a fraction, bringing her breasts into contact with his chest. "When it comes to you, I've never been satisfied."

She could feel his breath on her face. Her eyes drifted closed as she savored the increasing pressure of his body against hers. "Maybe that's the problem," she murmured. "I've been forbidden fruit for so long you think I'm something more than I really am."

"Maybe." He brushed his lips over hers once, twice.

She moaned.

"And maybe you have the same problem with me. Maybe you'd be disappointed."

"Maybe." Her breath came in shallow gasps.

He touched his tongue to her bottom lip. "We shouldn't be doing this."

"No."

His lips hovered, his breath warm and sweet. "Push me away."

"In a minute."

"Too late." He settled his mouth firmly over hers.

It was as good as she remembered. He'd taught her how to kiss years ago, and the master had only improved with age. His lips played, coaxed, drew responses from her she'd thought gone forever. She tunneled her fingers through his dark hair and opened her mouth to invite the thrust of his tongue, that wicked tongue that promised things she now understood. She grew damp with a woman's need many times more powerful than the vague longings she knew as a girl.

He pushed her coat from her shoulders and it slid into a crumpled semicircle around her. "I need to hold you," he murmured against her mouth.

Her reply came between kisses. "I need you, too." She pressed against the firm wall of his chest, her nipples tightening into buds aching for his touch.

"Oh, Meg." He cupped her breast and stroked her through the thin material of her dress.

"I've missed you, Luke," she whispered, arching into his caress.

He kissed her throat as his hand slipped inside the folds of the dress and found her breast. She gasped in response. He covered her mouth with his own and her world began to spin as it always had when Luke loved her. The musical whisper of the nearby fountain blended with the soft sounds of the night. And Luke was touching her again, as only he could. She pressed closer to his warmth. She needed this so much. She—

A car braked. Meg froze. A searchlight swept the area and her stomach clenched. *The police.*

5

LUKE SHIELDED MEG from the searchlight with his body. "Grab your coat," he muttered. Then he turned, keeping himself between Meg and the light, and shaded his eyes with one hand. "Good God, is that Bobby Joe I see before me?"

"Luke? Hell, I thought you were a couple of kids. Let me call off my backup." The tall policeman walked back to the squad car, switched off the searchlight and spoke into his walkie-talkie. When he returned he was smiling. "Sorry about that, but we patrol this area just to make sure nobody's pulling the kind of pranks you and I used to."

Meg had buttoned her coat and adjusted her hair by the time he arrived. She hoped the dim light would disguise her just-been-kissed look. "Hi, Bobby Joe," she said. "Luke and I were just touring the old spots. Didn't mean to startle you."

"Likewise." Bobby Joe shook hands with Luke. "It's been a long time."

"Too long, apparently." Luke grinned. "I come home after ten years and find Bobby Joe Harris decked out in a fuzz suit."

"Look who's talking!" Bobby Joe laughed and tapped Luke's vest. "The old Luke Bannister wouldn't have been caught dead in paisley."

"Yeah, well. Things have changed since the days we drag raced through town, buddy."

"Yeah." Bobby Joe hooked his thumbs in his belt. "I got two kids of my own already."

"I hope they give you just as much trouble as you gave your old man."

"They've already started." Static crackled from the squad-car radio and he glanced back toward the parking lot. "Hey, I gotta go," he said, holding out his hand to Luke. "Good seeing you. I'll be working a pop booth at the festival, so I'm sure we'll bump into each other again."

"Sure. See you." When Bobby Joe was out of earshot, Luke spoke in a low tone. "I'm sorry, Meg. What an idiot move on my part."

"Don't take all the blame on yourself. I'm responsible, too. God, I hope he didn't see anything." She touched her hair again. It was definitely coming loose from her careful arrangement. She groaned. "Even if he didn't, he could probably take one look at us and make an educated guess about what had been going on."

"Maybe. But he used to be the kind of guy who could keep his mouth shut."

"I hope you're right."

"Listen, if someone brings it up to you, tell them I lured you out here for my own devious plans. Tell them you were fighting me off when Bobby Joe showed up."

"Luke! I most certainly won't make up a story like that. It wouldn't work, anyway. I'm a terrible liar."

He looked into her eyes for a long moment. "In that case, you've just settled the question of what will happen, or rather, what *won't* happen when we get back to your house," he said quietly.

"What do you mean?"

"I saw you talking to Didi tonight. She knows I'm staying with you, doesn't she?"

"She guessed."

He tilted up her chin with his finger. "And if I know Didi, she'll ask a few leading questions tomorrow."

The banked fires of passion stirred to life. "She might."

His smile was both tender and sad. "I can't make love all night to a terrible liar, now can I?"

LUKE'S LOGIC was impeccable. Meg had to agree that whatever happened between them would be written all over her face for the whole town to see. She reminded herself of that over and over through the long, frustrating hours as Luke spent the night in the guest room and she stayed behind her own closed bedroom door. She lectured herself about the pitfalls of short-term happiness that sacrificed long-term goals.

She could walk down that hall and spend the rest of the night in Luke's arms. If she went, he wouldn't turn her away; she could only expect so much restraint from a mortal man. The hours would be filled with ecstasy, and in the morning she would emerge a changed woman. She might become a woman who dropped all responsibility in exchange for time with her lover. Luke had a powerful effect on her. She could easily blunder her duties for the ostrich festival, ruin all the months of preparation, and along with them her hopes of becoming chamber president.

So what? argued her passionate side. She could forget about her political ambitions and run off to Los Angeles with Luke. And be happy for a few weeks, maybe a few months, before her need to make a real difference in the world reasserted itself.

Her best, perhaps her only chance to realize that goal was to start here in Chandler, among the people who knew her. They held her ticket to the future, and it was the luck of the draw that they also held the keys to her imprisonment tonight. *Grow up*, she whispered into the darkness. *You need your rest*. But sleep wouldn't come, and the ache for Luke wouldn't leave.

DAWN SEEMED A LONG TIME arriving in the guest bedroom. When the dark sky turned the color of pearls, Luke dressed quickly in jeans, T-shirt and denim jacket. In the kitchen, Dog-breath wagged his tail and looked expectant.

"Sorry, boy. I can't take you. Wish I could." He left a note for Meg and headed off at a jog toward the Bannister farm. He had to straighten things out with Clint and convince his little brother to let him stay there. Luke couldn't spend another night under Meg's roof and keep away from her. Not after the way she'd responded at the high school last night. Some things were beyond a man's endurance, and keeping his hands off Meg after that brief taste of her passion was one of them.

A rooster crowed. He couldn't remember the last time he'd heard one. White-winged doves gathered on the telephone lines to watch his solitary passage down the deserted blacktop, and a cottontail scampered under a creosote bush by the side of the road. Luke slowed his pace and began to enjoy the cool morning air and the pale pink clouds at the horizon. Rural living had its moments.

Although he couldn't call the surrounding countryside strictly rural anymore. Some farms remained, and now and then a field contained a flock of sheep or a small herd of grazing dairy cattle. But now housing developments, some rising two stories, with bright red-tiled roofs, wedged themselves between the fields and changed the shape of the horizon. The way of life Luke remembered was slipping away.

The Bannister farmhouse hadn't changed much, just weathered to a lighter shade of gray. If Luke blocked out the cluster of houses about a mile down the road, the house looked almost picturesque in the pink light of dawn. The rising sun winked off the chrome bumper of Clint's candy-apple red truck. It was brand-new, as out of place on the run-down farm as a rose in a Dumpster. Luke could imagine what the payments were on a machine like that, but he understood why Clint had bought it. Clint's favorite toy when he was a kid had been a bright red truck.

Luke felt a tug of homesickness remembering the good times before his mother had died. He'd gather eggs from the henhouse first thing in the morning while his mother started bacon sizzling in a pan on the stove. In those days his father had helped with breakfast and had sung along with country and western songs playing on the kitchen radio while Clint set the table. His father had been musical. Luke had almost forgotten that. His guitar had been a birthday present when he was ten, and his dad had taught Luke his first chords.

Luke hadn't realized it was all so special, until the day his mother told him she had cancer. They'd all tried to keep the routine the same, but it proved impossible, and finally, when his mother had been too sick to stand, they'd given up the pretense. Luke wished his father had been stronger, but Orville Bannister had depended on his wife to keep him steady. When she died, he couldn't hold to the course. "We just aren't lucky, son," he'd told Luke as he slugged back another beer on the day of her funeral.

When Luke was forced to give up his relationship with Meg, he wasn't really surprised to have lost her. His father had lost the only woman he'd ever loved, and now Luke had, too. Bannister men were unlucky that way.

Apparently Clint wasn't faring any better. Debbie Fry might be a good-looking redhead, sweet in her way, but she was a party girl, not a potential wife for Clint. She'd been at least seven years behind Luke in school and five behind Clint, which made her barely twenty-one. Clint needed someone with more maturity if he ever expected to grow up himself.

Luke shook his head. Here he was passing judgment on his younger brother as if he had some right to do it.

That kind of attitude wouldn't get him very far with Clint.

He walked past the truck through a weed-choked side yard containing a split garden hose and a rusty wheelbarrow. Birds twittered and chirped in the feathery-leaved tamarisk trees that served as a windbreak for the house. The wooden steps leading to the kitchen door creaked when he mounted them. Several boards were warped and needed to be replaced. Luke tried the kitchen door. It was unlocked.

He poked his head inside. "Clint?" No answer. He stepped into the kitchen and grimaced at the pile of dirty dishes in the sink. His mother had kept the white Formica counters spotless. "Clint! It's me, Luke."

"Hold on." Clint came into the kitchen, barefoot and bare-chested, buttoning the fly of his jeans. He peered at Luke. "What you want?"

"To talk to you."

Clint glanced out the kitchen window. "You bring the whole town this time?"

"No, and I'm sorry about yesterday. I should have known there'd be some sort of—"

"Oh, but it just caught you by surprise, is that it? How modest of you."

"Clint, can we cut the crap and just talk? How about some coffee? I'll make it." He started toward the coffeepot.

"This isn't a good time. I got company."

Luke glanced back at Clint. "Debbie?"

"You been checking up on me or something?"

"I didn't think it was a secret."

"Clint?" Debbie appeared in the doorway, rubbing her eyes. She had on one of Clint's old western shirts and precious little else, it looked like. "How're you doin', Luke? I thought I heard somebody out here."

"Hi, Debbie." Luke couldn't fault his brother's taste. Debbie's long, shapely legs and cloud of red hair would excite most men. His first inclination was to ask if her mother knew where she was, but he restrained himself. A twenty-one-year-old was capable of making her own decisions about spending the night with a man.

Clint turned to her with a frown. "I think you'd better put some clothes on."

"I *have* clothes on." Debbie walked past him into the kitchen. "Have you offered Luke a cup of coffee or anything?"

"Luke can't stay. I'm sure he has all kinds of big-star things to do today, don't you, Luke?"

Luke sighed. "Later on I have to be at opening ceremonies, but right now I was hoping that we could—"

"Clint Bannister, you can at least give your brother a cup of coffee!" Debbie stood in the middle of the kitchen, her hands on her hips in such a way that the western shirt revealed a fair amount of bosom. "How do you like it, Luke? Black or with cream and sugar?"

Luke glanced at her and saw the spark of interest in her eyes. Damn. She was making a play for him in front of Clint. "Actually I don't feel much like coffee. Bad stomach this morning. I wanted to discuss some family matters with Clint, so if you'll excuse us . . ." He raised one eyebrow.

"Well, uh, okay." Debbie looked disappointed. "I'll just go take a shower, then, and get ready for work. I'm a teller at Valley National, down on the square, so if you should need any cash, just drop by and I'm sure we can—"

"Debbie." Clint scowled at her.

"Just trying to be neighborly, Clint." She flounced out of the room.

"Yeah, right." Clint gazed after her, and when he turned back to Luke, his gray eyes were hostile. "I suppose you get tired of that, women throwing themselves at you all the time."

"It's meaningless. They mix me up with my character and imagine I'm somebody I'm not."

"Don't give me that. This is your brother you're talking to, the one who got the leftovers, remember? I think they only dated me because they thought somehow, by hanging around me, they'd get a better chance at you."

"Clint, I don't want to fight with you. I'm not after Debbie, for God's sake."

"Doesn't matter. She's after you. I should have known last night when she asked where you were staying that she was hoping there'd be some brotherly get-togethers." He walked over to the sink, rinsed out a glass and filled it with tap water. "Nothing ever changes."

"A lot changes. You never used to hate me."

Clint took his time drinking the water. Then he put the glass down and wiped his mouth with the back of his hand. "You never used to be a jerk."

"Look, I know this celebrity stuff gets to you. I'm not crazy about it, either, but—"

"Are you kidding? You eat that garbage up. Just watching you makes me want to throw up."

Luke's jaw tightened. "Publicity's part of the job, but I can control it. I was hoping you'd let me stay here after all, Clint. The arrangement I have now isn't working, and besides, this thing between us is ridiculous. We're the only family either one of us has left, and we ought to be able to get along."

"Get along?" He gave a harsh laugh. "I'm not the one who waltzed off to California to lie on the beach, leaving my brother to cope with a drunken old man. I'm not the one who lives the life-style of the rich and famous, while my brother struggles to keep the friggin' cotton fields producing and the machinery working. It's not you who has to dicker with the cotton-gin people and pray that the price of cotton doesn't slip another notch."

"I *gave* you my share. Isn't that enough?"

"No, big brother, it's not half enough. But it does give me the right to tell you to get the hell out of *my* kitchen."

Luke clenched his fists, sorely tempted to take a swing at Clint. But that wouldn't solve anything. His brother saw only one side of the picture—his side. And right now, with his girlfriend singing in the shower down the hall, probably for Luke's benefit, Clint wouldn't be in the mood to see the other side. Without another word, Luke turned and walked out the kitchen door.

MEG WOKE UP FROM a light sleep when the back door closed. Luke had gone out, and she couldn't blame him. This was an impossible situation.

When Dog-breath scratched at her door, she threw on her robe and slippers and padded into the kitchen to feed him. She found Luke's note on the kitchen table, saying he'd gone to his brother's and would be back that afternoon in time for the opening ceremonies.

So Luke had gone to patch things up with Clint. He'd left on foot, too, considering the truck and car were still here. It wasn't far, maybe a little over two miles. She hoped they'd be able to work out some kind of truce, both for Luke's sake and for hers. If he and Clint could come to an understanding, then Luke could stay there as originally planned.

After putting Dog-breath in his run in the backyard, she showered and dressed in black jeans and an ostrich festival T-shirt. Her interview on the morning television news show wasn't until eleven, but if Luke came back early she wanted to be dressed, although she doubted that clothes would offer her protection against the sensual urges he inspired.

She wasn't hungry, but she forced down juice and toast to give her at least some fuel for the day. By eight the calls started coming in—last minute details that had to be settled. At ten she left for the station.

The interview started out well. Meg mentioned the names of the entertainers scheduled during the festival and the hours of the ostrich races. "And what about our grand marshal this year?" the show's host asked. "I've heard the women of Chandler are pretty excited to have Luke Bannister back in town."

Meg felt heat rise to her cheeks. Damn! "It's great to have a celebrity who grew up in Chandler as our grand marshal," she said.

"I understand you grew up here, too." The interviewer lifted an eyebrow. "Tell me, did Luke have a reputation with the ladies back then?"

Meg searched for a noncommittal answer while trying to calm her racing heart. "Luke's quite a guy," she said at last.

"And we'll look forward to seeing him in the parade on Saturday," the man said. The interview was over.

Meg escaped from the station and breathed in big gulps of fresh air to steady her nerves. Would people notice how flustered she'd become when the subject of Luke came up? She didn't doubt that a lot of people remembered she used to date him. She'd have to be careful when they next appeared in public together.

On her way home from the station Meg stopped by the neat clapboard house where she'd spent the first eighteen years of her life. She had to drop off two T-shirts for her parents, who had volunteered to help out during the festival. Meg needed all the bodies she could get, so she put aside her instincts to avoid her mother and father until after the weekend. She was furious about the way they'd interfered in her relationship with Luke, but didn't feel ready to discuss the matter while she was so preoccupied with the festival.

She went around to the back door as she had always done, and rapped once before entering the kitchen. "Mom?"

Nora Hennessy sat at the kitchen table eating a bowl of soup and watching a television program on the small under-cabinet model Meg's father had installed for her last Christmas. She was a small, trim woman with short, honey-colored hair, which had just started graying at the temples. She glanced at Meg with a startled expression. "Goodness! I didn't expect to see you on a busy day like this."

"Well, I just . . ." Meg paused as she became aware of the show her mother was watching. She glanced at the screen and back at her mother, who had the grace to blush. "*Connections*?" Meg asked, incredulous.

"It has a good story line."

"I didn't think you watched *any* soaps, let alone this one."

"Well, um, this is the only one I watch."

Meg stared at her mother. "I wasn't going to get into this, but it keeps hitting me in the face. Apparently you're one of Luke's secret fans, too."

Her mother's cheeks turned a deeper shade of pink. "I didn't say that."

"But you are, aren't you? I've heard how people talk about that show. Luke is the primary draw. People, or should I say *women*, don't watch it unless they're crazy about Dirk Kennedy." In the background she could hear Luke's voice. No wonder. He was on camera much of the time. And her mother watched him, just like a million other swooning women.

Nora picked up the remote beside her soup bowl and shut off the television. "There's nothing wrong with fantasy, Meg. The problem comes when you mix it up with real life."

"Is that what you thought I'd do? Is that why you didn't tell me Luke called here after he got the role in *Connections*?"

Nora seemed to have regained her composure. She rose from the table and started toward the pantry. "Sit down. I'll fix you some soup."

Meg tossed the T-shirts onto the kitchen table. "Actually I don't have time, but I'd love to have an answer to my question before I go."

"All right." Nora turned and faced her daughter. "Yes, I thought you'd leave Dan and run off to Hollywood if I gave you that message. Luke Bannister has always had that kind of influence on you, and your father and I have fought it every step of the way."

"I'm aware of your personal war against Luke," Meg said tightly. "I just found out Dad blackmailed him into breaking up with me in high school."

Tension lines bracketed her mother's mouth. "Obviously Luke's been telling you a few things. I hope that doesn't mean he's trying to work his way back into your life."

"Has it ever occurred to you that I might have been happy with Luke?"

"No." Her mother's voice remained steady. "If you thought about it logically, you'd agree. Luke's turned out better than your father and I expected, but his lifestyle is not for you. That big-city, glitzy style doesn't fit you at all. Besides that, you've wanted to be in politics for as long as I can remember, and this is the place to begin—the place where you grew up and have an established reputation. He's not going to leave California, and if you went there with him you'd be starting from scratch."

Meg took a deep breath. She couldn't bring herself to admit that her mother was right. "I just wish I'd been given the chance to make my own decisions about that."

"From the way you're talking, it sounds as if you still have a chance to make that decision."

Meg decided she'd rather not get into that with her mother. "I'd better go."

"Don't be foolish, Meg. He's an exciting man, but if he stood between you and your dream, the excitement would fade." Meg looked into her mother's eyes. "We love you, Meg. The Lord saw fit to bless us with only one child, so you're all we have. Your welfare has been our only concern since the day you were born."

"See you, Mom." Meg hurried out the door before she said something she'd regret and got herself into even more trouble.

From the frying pan into the fire, she thought as she drove to her house. Luke would surely be home by now, with opening ceremonies about two hours away. When she pulled the truck in the drive behind the BMW, she glanced into the side yard and noticed that her dog wasn't in his run. Evidently Luke was back. Taking a deep breath, she opened the front door. The sound of the shower and Luke singing confirmed that her nemesis had returned. Dog-breath glanced up from his position on the living-room rug and thumped his tail.

"You're enjoying this, aren't you?" she said, walking over to scratch behind the dog's ears. The trouble was, so was she. Driving home, knowing Luke would probably be there waiting for her, had been nerve-racking, but exciting, too. For the first time in nearly two years, she felt like a desirable woman, and it was a heady experience. She'd grown so accustomed to thinking of herself in nonsexual terms, as a widow, part owner of a business, a public servant. Luke had changed all that when he kissed her.

He obviously hadn't heard her come in. He was singing an old Rolling Stones tune about not getting any satisfaction. She sighed. That made two of them. Tossing her briefcase full of festival information on the couch, she walked into the kitchen for a glass of water. On the counter sat a bag of oranges, freshly picked, judging from the glossy stems and leaves still attached to some.

Surely he hadn't stolen them? She hoped not. This reliving the past stuff could get them both in hot water. But the oranges smelled good, and she hadn't eaten much all day. She took one from the bag and started peeling it over the sink.

"I thought I heard somebody rustling around in here."

She turned, the half-peeled orange in her hand. He stood in the doorway, toweling his hair. He had on a pair of the tightest jeans she'd ever seen on any human, and nothing else.

6

"DO YOU CARRY a permit for those?"

Luke draped the towel around his neck and glanced down at his skintight jeans. "My agent advised me to wear them."

Meg nodded. "Did he provide a bodyguard, too?"

"Shoot, this is the age of MTV. Nobody will blink an eye."

"I wouldn't bet on it." Her mother's words came back to her. *He's an exciting man.* Her mother didn't know the half of it. But apparently Luke took his sex appeal in stride, which might be the secret of his success. He was completely unself-conscious about his looks.

"I see you found the oranges."

She wrenched her gaze away from his well-developed chest and the curly dark hair she used to run her fingers through ten years ago. "Uh, yeah," she said, rediscovering the orange in her hand. "Where did they come from?"

He walked over to the table and rummaged through the bag. "Old man Peterson's tree."

"Luke, you didn't."

He picked out an orange and smiled at her. "Nah. I went over, knocked on the front door and talked to

Mrs. Peterson. Mr. Peterson died a few years back—I guess you knew that."

She nodded. How could she manage to stand in the same kitchen with this sexy man and not throw herself into his arms? She felt sticky juice running between her fingers. Glancing down at the orange she was unconsciously squeezing, she relaxed her grip. "Mrs. Peterson gave you these?"

"Traded is more like it. She needed her tree wells dug out a little, and we swapped my labor for a bag of oranges." Luke came over to the counter, tore off a paper towel from the holder, and began peeling the orange into it as he stood beside her. His clean skin gave off the vanilla scent of the soap he'd used, and his biceps bulged with each movement. "I went over there in the first place to apologize for stealing fruit when I was a kid."

"Did you apologize for me, too?"

"Not exactly. I told her I'd led you astray."

"I see." And he was threatening to do it again. She watched as he plucked the rind from the orange. Last night, he'd cupped her breasts in those same hands. She wanted him to touch her again.

"She acted like she didn't even know I'd gone away." He glanced at Meg. "That took me down a notch or two, in case I was getting above my raising, as they say."

"You're not cocky, Luke."

"Tell that to my brother." He poked a section of orange into his mouth and chewed. "Great. Just like I remember."

"What happened with your brother?"

"Well, he—" Luke glanced at the orange in her hand. "You gonna eat that or hold it?"

"I'm going to eat it." She dutifully peeled the rest of the orange and put a slightly crushed section into her mouth. She ate the orange without tasting it, her heart pounding as fantasies of loving him swirled through her mind.

"Clint has a real chip on his shoulder, Meg. He pictures me as living the good life in California while he slaves away on the farm. I guess he's forgotten I had to learn how to survive on my own while he stayed here in familiar territory and was handed a farm. All he sees is that he has it tough and I have a glamorous career."

"That's too bad." Meg's orange got messier, and she had to lean over the sink to keep the juice from dripping onto her shirt. Still, some splattered. "Darn it."

"Here." Luke grabbed the dishrag draped over the faucet and dabbed at the spot just above her left breast. "I didn't mean for you to get—"

"Luke." She caught his hand, her heart racing. "For God's sake."

He went very still and his blue eyes turned smoky. He didn't move his hand, and the dampness of the dishrag chilled her heated skin. "I thought about you every minute of today," he said softly. "Walking along the roads we used to walk along, seeing the old places where we used to play hide-and-seek, the mesquite grove where we built the fort, the irrigation ditch where we went swimming. You were everywhere."

She couldn't move, couldn't speak.

He opened his hand, and the dishrag fell to the floor. He stroked the side of her neck before sliding his hand beneath her hair and cradling her head. "I've missed you so much. I need you, Meg," he whispered, and lowered his lips to hers.

She rested her trembling hands against his chest and he shuddered. He was so warm. She breathed in his familiar scent mingled with the sharp sweetness of oranges. The taste of oranges flavored their kiss as he took possession of her mouth.

She spread her fingers and combed them up though the luxurious pelt covering his chest. *Luke.* His name eddied through her consciousness. When she wound her arms around his neck, he pulled her close. She pressed against the firm mound beneath the tight denim of his jeans and her body responded with an aching rush of moisture. He thrust his tongue deep into her mouth. She yielded to him, mindless of anything but the melding of their bodies.

Then with a groan he released her. "I wasn't going to do this!"

Dazed and breathless, she opened her eyes and steadied herself with one hand against the counter. He was breathing hard, and his gaze was filled with agony. She struggled to speak and finally got the words out. "But you see, I'm as much to blame. I want you, too."

"No, you don't. Maybe now, at this very moment, but later you'd be sorry. I don't want to louse things up for you this weekend, Meg. I really don't. I tried to get Clint to let me sleep there, but he won't listen to reason. And if I stay here with you another night we'll make love. I can guarantee it."

She glanced away and took a deep breath. "You won't be staying here. I checked with the San Marcos this morning and they were able to make some adjustments and book you into a suite. We can move your things over as soon as you're ready."

"Good. That's good."

She glanced back at him. "I wish I hadn't done it, Luke."

Desire blazed in his eyes for a moment, and then he seemed to deliberately snuff it out. "It's the right decision. Let's get me packed up and out of your life while I still have some self-control."

THEY TOOK THE BMW into town, although Luke said he was resigned to the paparazzi picking up his trail again once the opening ceremonies took place.

"The San Marcos will keep your room number confidential," Meg said as she took a back road around the hotel's golf course to avoid the crowded square. "As long as you can keep that photographer from following you to your room, and I'm sure the staff will help you with that, you should be able to have some privacy at the hotel."

He glanced at her. "It doesn't really matter. I'm public property from now until Sunday, anyway."

"I guess so." She felt irritable and possessive. He'd added boots and a blue satin Western shirt to his tight jeans, and she didn't want him to be public property looking like that. She swung the BMW into the circular drive in front of the hotel.

"Come to think of it, you're public property now, too," he added.

But no one would be pawing her, she thought. "Luke, I wish—"

"Hey." He touched her arm. "You have a job to do. I understand that."

"Do you?"

His smile was rueful. "As long as there's a safe distance between us," he said, looking into her eyes. "But when you're in my arms, I turn into this selfish guy who only wants—"

A valet opened the passenger door. "May I take your luggage, Mr. Bannister?"

Luke turned to the valet. "Sure." Then he glanced back at Meg and winked. "Showtime," he said softly and got out of the car.

She watched him walk into the lobby and draw the attention of every woman along the way. If only she could turn the clock back. For twenty-four hours she'd had him all to herself. She hadn't cherished those moments nearly enough.

THE NEXT HOUR WAS A BLUR. Meg picked up the walkie-talkie that would be her constant companion for the next few days and the green John Deere utility cart she'd use to drive around the festival grounds. She checked to make sure the streets surrounding the festival area had been roped off before heading back to the San Marcos to pick up Luke.

When she found him in the lobby, he was surrounded by autograph seekers. As she maneuvered into the crowd and signaled to him that it was time to leave, she wished his agent had sent bodyguards. Getting him to the utility cart took skill, diplomacy and some deft moves. She waved him into the seat beside her and slid in behind the wheel. Snapping on her walkie-talkie, she lifted it to her mouth. "This is Meg. We're on our way."

Luke glanced at her and grinned. "Reminds me of the dune buggy Bobby Joe used to have. Don't pretend this isn't fun, driving this puppy around."

Meg grinned back as she steered a course between food booths and arts and crafts displays. "Okay, it's fun."

The festival grounds hummed with anticipation. Food vendors stoked up popcorn poppers and electric grills while carts delivering bags of ice zipped past. Craft booths were crowded with wind chimes and bola ties, jewelry and original art. The candy colors and serpentine loops of the carnival stood silent and poised for action after the opening ostrich race at five, and a legion of stuffed animals hung ready to be claimed by anyone who could accurately pitch a quarter, a softball or a dart.

Meg pulled in next to the yellow-and-white-striped VIP tent set up at one end of the oval racetrack where the ostriches, llamas and camels would run. Parked next to the tent were the livestock tractor trailers that had brought the animals to Chandler. Bleachers at the opposite end and along one side were already filled, and the overflow crowd sat on a grassy hill opposite the bleachers. Service-club members hawked beer and soft drinks to the crowd while country music blared from loudspeakers.

"This is quite an operation," Luke said as he climbed out of the cart and followed Meg into the tent, where chamber of commerce members and city officials were sampling a colorful buffet.

"It has to be. If the festival doesn't go well, we'll struggle all year to fund our community programs."

"They've entrusted you with a big responsibility."

Meg laughed. "If I screw this up, I'll have to leave town. Come on, let's get something to eat before it's too late."

After they moved through the buffet she quickly lost track of Luke as people jockeyed for his time and attention. The tent area was off-limits to general spectators, but Meg noticed the paparazzi hanging around. She still wore her Dodgers cap on backward, but she'd changed into a long-sleeved shirt and bib overalls.

Meg worried that the young woman might try to sneak into the gathering. When Bobby Joe drove up in a utility cart just like hers, she walked over to talk with him. He was out of uniform, helping the service club with beer and soft-drink sales, but Meg had never known him to be truly off duty.

Meg glanced back at the photographer. Then, turning to Bobby Joe, she said, "I'd like to make sure that woman with all the cameras stays out of here."

"Sure thing." Bobby Joe adjusted his sunglasses. "How's it going?"

"Everything seems to be fine." She gazed at him, but couldn't see his eyes through the sunglasses. "About Wednesday night, Bobby Joe, I—"

"Hey." He held up one large hand. "That's your business, Meg."

The knot of anxiety loosened. "Then you didn't make a report or anything?"

"Why should I? You and Luke are both my friends. Consider it forgotten."

Meg sighed with relief. "Thanks, Bobby Joe."

"No problem."

Meg returned to the crowd of city officials. The air seemed more balmy now, the mood more festive. She'd made a mistake, but fortunately the mistake had been discovered by someone with loyalty and consideration. Her reputation was still intact.

The owner of the racing ostriches took the center of the arena, and called for attention over the loudspeakers. Meg tensed, knowing what was coming next. The man ran through his usual speech of being happy to be back with the fine folks of Chandler. Then he paused. "This year we have a new wrinkle in the program. The Chandler Chamber of Commerce is auctioning off a date with the parade grand marshal, who is none other than local celebrity and star of *Connections*, Luke Bannister!"

The crowd cheered and Luke went to the front of the tent and waved.

"The winner will be picked up in a limo, driven to the San Marcos to have dinner with Luke in the Nineteen-Twelve restaurant, presented with a dozen roses and given unlimited rides at the carnival. So, if I can have one of my assistants draw from this bowl of names, we'll find out who the lucky lady is."

Meg held her breath. She didn't want anybody going on a date with Luke. No matter that the raffle had raised a sizable amount of money for the chamber or that it would generate some good publicity for Luke. She hated the idea.

"And the winner is . . ." The announcer paused for dramatic effect. "Debbie Fry!"

A shriek went up from the bleachers and Debbie bounded down waving her arms. "Yes!" she cried, "yes, yes, yes!"

"I think she's happy about it," the announcer said. "Now, Miss Fry, if you'll go over to the VIP tent and identify yourself, Luke Bannister will know who he's taking out Friday night. I would say he's a lucky man."

Meg forced herself to meet Debbie and congratulate her. Luke stepped forward with a smile and said he was delighted to be her escort the following night. Meg suspected he was acting again, but still, her insides twisted with jealousy. She wasn't proud of the emotion, but it had her firmly in its grip.

Flash! Meg was temporarily blinded by the flare of light. Through the black spots dancing in front of her eyes she saw the paparazzi moving away. Meg felt certain she'd been in the shot. She hoped her emotions hadn't shown on her face. She could imagine the tabloid gossip now: "Former girlfriend watches jealously as Luke charms new woman." No, she was becoming paranoid. The photographer had no interest in her. Meg had just been in the way.

The first ostrich race began, with three ostriches pulling small chariots in red, white and blue. The drivers wore Roman helmets and sweeping capes in matching colors. The crowd laughed and cheered as the ostriches nearly ran into each other circling the track with their prancing, long-legged gait. Meg faked some enthusiasm; in the past she'd been fascinated by the huge, swift-footed birds with their long plumes and backward-folding knees. But from the corner of her eye she could see Debbie smiling up at Luke and Luke smiling back. Meg gritted her teeth.

Thankfully a call came in on her walkie-talkie. Something had gone wrong with the giant bubble-gum machine set up by the crafts booths. Meg went over and told Luke he was on his own for a while, and sped off in her utility cart.

CLINT DROVE his newly washed truck over to Debbie's house at six-thirty that night. They had a date for the carnival, although after the scene that morning with Luke, he didn't relish taking Debbie anywhere his brother might happen to be. But all Clint's buddies were taking their wives and girlfriends to the carnival tonight, and Clint didn't want to miss the fun. Luke just better stay the hell away from Debbie, and vice versa.

Debbie rented a little guest house behind her parents' place, which was why he and Debbie always ended up at his house. The guest house was too close to her mom and dad for Clint's comfort when he was enjoying the charms of their daughter.

Debbie came out the front door as soon as he drove up. He liked that about her—she watched for him and was always on time. His gaze flicked appreciatively over her tight lavender jeans and pink blouse. She wore the collar of the blouse turned up and the shirttails tied at her waist. Clint thought she looked sexy as hell. The guys would sure envy him tonight.

He leaned over and opened the passenger door. When she climbed in, he took a deep breath of her perfume. "You smell great, sugar."

"Thanks." She didn't look at him.

"Got a kiss for me?"

"Sure." She leaned over and kissed him quickly, without putting much feeling into it.

"Hey." He grabbed her and pulled her close for a good long soul kiss. Then he let her go and put the truck in gear. "That's better."

Usually she talked a mile a minute when she got in the truck, but tonight she was quiet, letting the country music from the radio fill the silence.

His curiosity grew. "Something wrong, sugar?"

She glanced at him nervously. "I guess I'd better tell you. You'll find out pretty quick, anyway."

His stomach churned. This had something to do with Luke; he just knew it. "So tell me."

"I won the raffle."

"What raffle?" He had no idea what she was talking about.

"The one for a date with your brother."

"What?" Clint veered to the side of the road and slammed on the brakes. He felt sick. "You actually bought a ticket?"

"Twenty."

His shoulders sagged. Of course she'd bought twenty tickets. Who was he kidding? All along she'd gone out with him because he was Luke Bannister's brother. And now that Luke was around, who needed him?

"It's just for one night," she said, her voice softer, less defiant. "Friday."

He straightened and gazed out the windshield as he assessed the damage. To be honest, he wasn't in love with Debbie. But he liked her a lot, and she was known around town as his steady girl. She might not break his heart if she ran off with Luke, but she'd sure knock a hole in his pride. Damn Luke. Why couldn't he have stayed where he belonged?

Debbie's question was barely audible. "Are we still going to the carnival tonight?"

Clint shoved the truck into gear. "You're damn right."

"You're mad, aren't you?"

The tires squealed as Clint turned a corner. "Nah. Not old Clint."

LACK OF SLEEP was beginning to catch up with Meg, but she couldn't go home just yet. People still needed to consult with her, and Didi said there was a problem with one of the entries in the parade. Meg drove her cart toward the command tent the festival committee used.

Since the opening ceremonies she hadn't seen much of Luke, at least not in the flesh. A giant-screen television had been set up near the row of arts and crafts booths, and it featured continuous footage of *Connections*. Occasionally Meg would walk past and catch a glimpse of Luke, twice his normal size, bending over whatever woman he was bedding during that particular episode. She always had to turn away, just as someone on a diet might have to ignore the dessert menu.

She'd almost reached the tent when Luke suddenly stepped in front of the cart. She had to brake quickly to avoid hitting him.

"Park that thing and come with me."

"What's wrong?"

"I need to talk to you. Come on."

She wheeled the cart into an empty space between two booths and climbed out. "Is it that photographer? The baby ostrich? What?"

"I'll tell you on the Ferris wheel. It's the only spot in this crazy place where we can be alone."

"Luke, I don't like the Ferris wheel."

"I'll protect you."

He'd never forced her on a carnival ride back in high school, but tonight he seemed desperate enough to drag her there. "I could get sick all over you."

"Trust me. You won't get sick." They reached the ride and Luke motioned to the ticket taker, who waved them to the head of the line.

"Guess it helps to be Dirk Kennedy, huh?" someone called out.

"Always," Luke said, and flashed a smile. Several people asked for autographs. "When I get back," he promised, and handed Meg into one of the swinging cars.

Her stomach lurched. "This is not a good idea."

"It's a great idea."

The car started forward as the wheel began its slow grinding upward motion, lifting them higher off the ground. "Oh, Luke." Meg's stomach felt as if someone had dropped a stone into it. She gripped the handrail.

"You'll be fine." He took her hands between both of his. "Look at me."

She did, and immediately began to relax. Who could think of anything terrible looking into eyes the color of the Arizona sky? And such gentle eyes. The wheel carried them upward, but she kept gazing into his eyes and didn't feel the least bit sick.

He smiled. "That's better. I knew you could do it."

Then she made the mistake of looking down at the kaleidoscope of lights below her and almost passed out. "Oh, my God."

"Look at me."

She held on to his gaze like a talisman and her stomach stopped quivering.

"Just keep looking at me, then. I like that better, anyway."

"This is almost like being hypnotized, Luke."

"Hey, I never thought of trying that."

She chuckled. "It would be overkill."

"Oh, Meg, what I wouldn't give..." He sighed. "Time to change the subject. I brought you up here to see if we can do anything about this date with Debbie Fry."

"Do? Do what? What's wrong?"

"She's Clint's girl."

"I know, but she won the raffle legitimately, and you saw how excited she was. I can't imagine trying to talk her out of it."

"You're sure? Because I thought maybe, if you offered her the roses and the limo ride and the dinner, to be used with Clint instead of me, then we could choose somebody else for the date. I'd cover the extra expense."

"I can try, but I saw her face, Luke. She may be Clint's girl, but she wants that date with you."

"Damn." He smiled sadly. "I was even fantasizing that you could rig it so that you could go on the date with me."

"Wouldn't work. I'd be run out of town on a rail."

"No, you wouldn't, because I'd ride in and save you, like Lancelot did with Guinevere when they were going to burn her at the stake."

"You always were a romantic."

"Yeah. Did you know we've made three complete circles and you haven't been sick yet?"

Meg chuckled. "Now *that's* romantic."

"And now we've stopped on the very top, my favorite spot."

She kept her gaze fastened on his, but her stomach still gave a little flip. "Don't tell me where we are. I don't want to know."

"There's a tradition about stopping at the top of the wheel. Of course you wouldn't know about it, because you won't ride in one."

"If it has something to do with rocking the car like crazy, we can forget tradition."

"That's one tradition. This is the other one." He took her face between his hands and kissed her. It was a soft kiss, undemanding and sweet. He pulled back and gazed into her eyes. "Do you like that tradition?"

She felt as if she were floating. "You're crazy."

"Let's kiss until we start moving. Nobody can see us up here."

"This is dangerous, Luke."

"Only if you attack me and start ripping my clothes off. If you can control yourself, we'll be fine."

She laughed, and he kissed her while her mouth was slightly open. His tongue slipped inside, and her heart hammered in her chest. What was she doing, recklessly kissing him like this? But she couldn't stop. He tasted so good, and she needed the pressure of his lips, the clever thrust of his tongue.

The car started with a jolt, and he drew back to gaze at her. "Maybe you'd better try frowning or something."

"Why?"

"Because right now you look like a woman who wants to make love."

"It's your fault."

"Frown at me."

She frowned, and then started laughing again. She was still laughing when they stepped out of the car and the camera flashed in her face.

7

"I HAVE TO GO," Meg said, releasing Luke's hand and hurrying away. She glanced over her shoulder to see fans surrounding Luke and the paparazzi taking more shots. Meg shrugged away her concern. What could someone do with a picture like that? It was hardly incriminating. All the incriminating action had taken place off camera.

She hastened back to her cart and drove to the festival command tent. After finishing her business there, she thought about trying to find Debbie in the crowd, but her walkie-talkie crackled again and she was off to find a replacement light for one of the soft-drink booths. One chore led to another until finally the rides and booths started closing down for the night. Meg figured Debbie had gone home. She'd have to catch her at the bank in the morning. Meg doubted she'd give up her date with Luke, anyway.

For a moment, Meg allowed herself to imagine a double date with Clint and Debbie, Luke and her. Just like old times, except Debbie hadn't been the girl on Clint's arm back then. She'd been far too young, still in grade school. She wasn't too young now, and Meg hated the thought of Luke's hand in hers, his arm draped around her shoulders. Would Luke kiss her good-night? Would he do more than that? Of course not. The thought was unworthy. And yet, he was a hot-blooded man, and he had no strings....

THE NEXT MORNING she found Luke over by the petting zoo, where Dirk Kennedy, the baby ostrich, was the main attraction. People wanted pictures of Luke with his character's namesake. Luke's jeans weren't as tight as yesterday's, but he made up for that with a wide-sleeved, collarless white shirt unbuttoned almost to the waist, and knee-high leather moccasins that accentuated the curve of his calves. Dark glasses made him look like a mysterious and dangerous pirate. Somebody sure knew how to dress him to advantage.

Meg caught his attention and signaled to him. In a few minutes he excused himself and walked over to where she stood in the shade of the auto-show tent. He pulled off his sunglasses and smiled when he reached her. "You look terrific. And you smell a lot better than the petting zoo."

"You're an old farm boy. You should be used to a little manure."

"Actually I'm having a good time. In fact, seeing you here makes my day complete."

"Thanks." She looked into those blue, blue eyes and her concentration disappeared.

"Did you need me for something?"

Yes. She forced herself back to reality. "I drove over to the bank just now and talked to Debbie. She wants to go through with the date tonight."

He squinted off into the distance and twirled the sunglasses. "That's too bad."

"I suggested she use the whole package with Clint instead of you." Meg's gaze wandered to the open shirt and the dark chest hair it revealed. "Debbie said going out with Clint instead of you would be stupid."

"I don't know what she expects. I plan to treat her the way I'd treat a little sister if I had one."

"I doubt she expects that."

He gazed down at Meg. "As they say in the old songs, if I can't have you, I don't want nobody else."

Her pulse raced. She loved hearing words like that, even if she didn't quite believe them. On Sunday he'd go back to L.A., and she couldn't picture Luke staying celibate for long. "Well, let's hope Debbie has a nice time with someone who acts like her older brother."

"She won a date, not a seduction."

Meg smiled. "You sound a little testy."

"Frustration can do that to a man." Then he gave her a quick grin. "But I can handle it, and Debbie, and my little brother, if it comes to that. I see how important all of this is to you. I don't want to mess it up." He watched a couple of kids walk by with sticky pink goo all over their mouths and two empty cardboard tubes. "Say, can I buy you some cotton candy for old times' sake?"

"It's a nice thought, but I have a million things to do. Incidentally, a TV crew is coming tonight to film you and Debbie enjoying the carnival."

"Okay. And thanks for trying to change her mind about the date."

"Sure." She watched him walk away and gather people like filings to a magnet. She understood. He pulled at her that way every time she come near him.

THAT EVENING THERE WERE no major problems erupting at the festival, so Meg decided to work at the chamber of commerce beer concession near the entertainment pavilion. Traditionally it had been the busiest, most boisterous place at the festival, so Meg hoped she wouldn't have time to think about Luke and his date with Debbie.

She managed to keep them at the back of her mind until the moment they arrived at the festival and walked right past the beer truck. Luke sported a dark Western suit that emphasized his broad shoulders, while Debbie wore a slinky silver number that glistened with each sinuous step. She carried her bouquet of roses in one arm and looped the other one firmly though Luke's. As they walked she kept bumping into him and leaning her cheek against his shoulder.

The paparazzi was energetically getting the couple on film. Debbie posed and pouted for the camera as if she were a budding starlet. Meg remembered vaguely that acting was Debbie's ambition, so of course she'd make the most of tonight. Still, the sight of Debbie draped all over Luke gave Meg a headache. The only thing that helped was Luke's unguarded expressions. For the most part he smiled and looked pleasant, but Meg noticed one moment when he projected total boredom.

Luke and Debbie walked in the direction of the entertainment pavilion where a well-known Southern rock group was playing. They were nearly out of Meg's line of vision when Clint stepped into their path. He was weaving. Meg yelled at one of the other workers to take over her station and ran out the back of the booth.

As she raced toward the cluster of people gathering around Luke, Debbie and Clint, she imagined disaster. The televison crew was due any minute. Luke in the midst of a brawl would embarrass everyone.

Clint stood, feet apart, in front of Luke and Debbie. "I see you got yourself a sweet young thing, brother," he drawled.

"Back off, Clint. Debbie and I are just doing our part for charity."

"Yeah. That little gal can be real charitable."

"How dare you?" Debbie started forward, hand raised.

Luke pulled her back. "Let me handle him." Debbie looked adoringly at Luke and moved back to give the brothers room. Luke stepped toward Clint and lowered his voice. "Watch your step, little brother. Debbie's a terrific woman, but she's a friend, and that's all. Don't make this into something ugly."

Clint jabbed a finger at Luke. "Don't pull that high and mighty act on me. This is your brother, Lukey-boy. I was around when Dad tanned your bare butt with a willow switch because you were getting too friendly with the girls in the neighborhood. You've never met a woman you didn't want. I know you. But Debbie's my girl. Stay away from her."

"I'm not anybody's girl," Debbie called out from the sidelines.

Meg saw the television crew approaching from the right. For a moment she stood rooted to the spot, unsure of what to do and dreading Luke's reaction to his brother's defiant confrontation.

Luke's eyes narrowed. "Go home and sleep it off, Clint."

"Make me, pinup boy."

Luke's hands clenched and a muscle in his jaw twitched. Meg, reacting instinctively, pushed through the crowd and grabbed Luke's arm. She felt as if she'd latched on to a corded steel cable. "Don't," she whispered. "Please."

A shudder coursed through him. He gazed down at her, and she had trouble believing eyes so filled with anger could have looked at her so lovingly the night before.

"You could ruin the festival. Don't fight," she pleaded. Slowly the fire faded and the gentleness returned. The muscles in his arms relaxed. "Thank you, Luke," she murmured.

"Is loverboy backing down?" Clint taunted.

"I won't fight you," Luke said. "Let's go, Debbie." He held out his hand and started back the way they'd come.

"Chicken-livered son of a bitch!" Clint yelled. "I know why you won't fight. You're afraid of messing up that pretty-boy face of yours!"

Meg held her breath as Luke paused and his shoulders tensed. He glanced over at her, took a deep breath and grinned. Then he mouthed the word "showtime" and guided Debbie off toward the carnival.

Clint tried to run after him, but a couple of his friends held him back. Shaking, Meg leaned against the nearest booth for support. That was all she needed—to have a parade grand marshal with a black eye and broken nose.

The television reporter approached her. "Are you Meg O'Brian?"

She nodded.

"Wasn't Luke Bannister the guy arguing with somebody?"

"Luke's on his way over to the carnival," Meg said. "If you hurry you should be able to catch him."

"Well, what was that argument all about?"

Meg forced a smile. "Absolutely nothing."

The reporter stared doubtfully at her for a moment and finally shrugged. "If you say so. Come on, guys, we have a midway to film."

LUKE STOOD WITH DEBBIE on the outskirts of the crowd listening to a slow, sexy song the band had pushed to number one on the charts a few months ago. Some couples were dancing in the soft grass. Debbie had suggested they do the same, but he'd made an excuse about not being a good dancer. He turned his wrist just a fraction to look at the time. Another half hour and he could reasonably call this date over. He could hardly wait.

When he'd agreed to go along with this idea of a "Date with Dirk," he'd thought it would be no big deal. He'd taken out his share of women for promotional purposes, and this would be the same thing. Except that yesterday he'd held Meg in his arms, and now the touch of any other woman grated against his skin. Debbie's perfume assaulted him with its stridency, and her voice was pitched in the wrong key. He wanted Meg.

He was beginning to understand the spot he'd put himself in by coming back here. Over the years Meg had evolved into a fantasy figure, still desirable, but not an obstacle in his pursuit of pleasure with other women. Now she'd moved into the forefront again, and no other woman could be an acceptable substitute after holding her. Since he couldn't have Meg, his love life was going to be in big trouble. Maybe in another ten years he'd forget her sufficiently to enjoy other women. Then again, maybe not.

Debbie linked her arm through his and snuggled closer. "You're wonderful, Luke."

He eased away from her blatant attempt at intimacy. "I'm just a guy."

"I'm beginning to wonder about that." There was an edge to her voice. "I usually don't have any trouble encouraging a man to make a move. And I've heard you have a reputation with women. So what's wrong, Luke? Don't you find me attractive?"

He looked into her pale blue eyes. "You're very attractive, Debbie." He wondered how much he dared say. Even a suggestion that there was someone else might cast suspicion on Meg. They had been seen together a lot, and no telling if Bobbie Joe would keep his mouth shut.

"You haven't even kissed me once."

He smiled. "I don't think that was part of the raffle."

"We could make it part of the raffle. If you want."

A week ago he would have accepted the invitation in those half-closed eyes, those parted lips. But last night he'd kissed Meg at the top of the Ferris wheel, and he could still feel what that was like. He didn't want other lips messing with his recollection. "I'm sorry, Debbie."

"You're sure nothing like your brother."

"You'd probably have been better off with him tonight."

"Clint's okay, but he's not going anywhere with his life. He's a dead-end street. If I stay with him, I'll be stuck here, too."

"Ah." He should have figured out her motivation sooner. It could have saved them both a lot of time. "I guess you want to know if I can help you with contacts in Hollywood."

"Of course not!" Her expression turned sulky. "I just want to get to know you better, but you won't let me."

"Debbie, you don't have to be coy. I'd be glad to help you if I can. You look like you'd be photogenic. I can't promise anything, but I could talk to some people, see about an audition for *Connections*."

"You could? That would be *great*."

"In return, I want you to tell Clint that nothing happened between us tonight. In fact, I'd appreciate your spreading the word that I was a perfect gentleman."

She frowned and cocked her head to one side. "I don't know. That kind of makes me look bad, you know, that you didn't try anything."

"Then say I was coming down with a head cold or something, and you didn't want to catch it." He sighed. "I'd just like to get Clint off my case on at least this one issue."

"So you'll do this for me, and I don't have to sleep with you or anything?"

"Surprise, surprise."

"Not that it would have been so *horrible* if I had. My girlfriends would all have been jealous if I'd gone to bed with Luke Bannister."

"Just remember that stuff on-screen isn't real. Like I said, I'm just a guy."

"Then all the stories I heard about you in high school aren't true?"

"Gross exaggerations. Come on, let's go find that kid we paid to hold your flowers."

A half hour later, Luke put Debbie in the limo and walked back to the San Marcos. Thank God that was over. Debbie was happy, but Clint was still one screwed-up guy. He hoped Debbie's description of her night out with him would make a difference. Luke didn't want the difficulties between him and his brother to get any worse. In fact, before he left Chandler he'd like to iron out a few of them.

When he got back to his suite the message light was blinking. He called the front desk and retrieved the message from his agent Henry Davis. The message said "Screen test on Monday."

Screen test. He finally had a shot at a movie part, the one he and Henry had hoped would come through. This could be the biggest career break he'd had since landing the part in *Connections*.

He wanted to tell somebody, to rejoice with somebody, but who? He could call some of his friends back in L.A., but most of them were sitting around waiting for the same break. It would be like rubbing salt in their wounds. Clint wouldn't care. But Meg—Meg would be happy for him, even though his career was one of the reasons they were being forced apart.

Luke remembered the time he'd won a new bike by entering a contest on the back of a cereal box. Clint had been jealous, but Meg had whooped with joy. Then she'd managed to bring Clint around, convincing him that he'd benefit because he'd get Luke's old bike, and she'd help him paint it to look brand-new. Even back then Meg had been a little politician, Luke thought with a smile.

Maybe, just maybe, she was the key to this trouble with Clint. She might even be able to act as a go-between, get them back on track. He picked up the phone by the bed and dialed her number. He got her machine and put a message on it for her to call. He left his extension.

WHEN SHE GOT HOME, Meg played her messages from the answering machine in her bedroom. When Luke's voice came on, she automatically took down the number and the extension. Then she stared at the pad of paper as the machine beeped and whirred back to its starting position. Whether he'd meant to or not, Luke had just given her his room number.

She hadn't wanted the information and had deliberately not listened when the clerk at the San Marcos had told her. Luke hadn't mentioned it, either. But now here it was, as if written in neon, flashing at her from the page. And he wanted her to call. Or so he said. Was this really an invitation?

She paced the bedroom floor and wrestled with longings that threatened to hurl her out the door and into Luke's arms. Then she thought of an explanation for his leaving the extension number for her. If she'd called and asked for Luke, the desk had instructions not to put people through. If she didn't have the extension number, she wouldn't be able to call him back. He'd had no hidden agenda. He just wanted to talk to her.

More disappointed than relieved, she dialed the number. He picked it up on the second ring. "Hi, it's me," she said, in the same way they'd indentified themselves to each other ten years ago.

"Hi, me." He fell into the same pattern.

"What's going on?"

"Well, for one thing, my agent called and I have a screen test on Monday for the movie part I've been trying to get."

"Luke, that's wonderful!" The news was bittersweet. Now he'd really be lost to her. But she could imagine how much he'd wanted this break. "By the way, thanks for keeping cool tonight with Clint. I guess it's just as well you didn't fight and risk bruising your face right before this screen test."

"Yeah, I guess so. Listen, it's Clint I really called about. I need to talk to him—someplace where nobody else can butt in. When I first arrived, the whole damn town was there, and when I went over to the house the next morning, Debbie was hanging around. I think if he and I could sit down with no distractions, we might be able to get some things talked out."

"Could be." Meg wasn't so sure. She'd seen the look on Clint's face tonight.

"You've always been good at being our go-between. Could you get a message to him tomorrow that I'll be alone in my room after the festival, and that I'd like him to come over for a beer or something? Do you think he'd come?"

"He might." Meg heard the hope in Luke's voice and her heart ached for him. Clint probably missed Luke, too, but he was so pigheaded he'd never admit it.

"Debbie promised to tell Clint nothing happened between us tonight. I'm hoping that will help."

"Uh, yeah, it could." She felt her own personal victory at his announcement. "Did you . . . have a good time, at least?"

"No."

"I'm sorry...no, I take that back. I'm not sorry at all. I hated the idea of you and Debbie out together."

"Maybe almost as much as I did."

Meg closed her eyes and pictured him in the dark Western suit over a crisp white shirt, and underneath that—just Luke. She wanted him so much.

"Meg?"

"I'm here. I'm just . . ."

"I know."

"It's stupid of me, Luke. We can't be together, and that's that."

He hesitated. "Yeah," he said at last.

"So let's hang up and go to sleep."

"I miss you, Meg."

"I miss you, too." Slowly she placed the receiver in its cradle and stood by the phone, willing it to ring, hoping he'd need her too much for caution.

8

AT NINE-THIRTY SATURDAY morning Meg wound her way through the floats, convertibles and horseback riders gathered on Arizona Avenue two miles from the center of town. She wanted to make sure Didi wasn't having any problems with other entries.

She passed the Chandler High School Band, resplendent in blue and white. The horn section gleamed in the sun as band members ran through scales. Drummers marched in place practicing their staccato parade rhythm, and the pep squad rustled blue-and-white pom-pons in time to the beat. Meg caught the sense of excitement as she moved past prancing horses and crepe paper-covered floats. The air smelled of farm animals, gasoline fumes and the freshly cut wood used to build the floats.

Before she found Didi, she spotted her parents' decorated buckboard. They'd driven the buckboard in each of the ostrich festival parades, with her mother dressed in a long gingham dress and bonnet for added effect. Her mother stood watching as her father struggled with a harness on one of the horses.

Meg glanced down at her white slacks and blazer. She was wearing an ostrich festival T-shirt underneath, but she'd dressed up a little more today in honor of the parade. If she helped her father, she'd probably get dirt all over her outfit. Meg's mother caught sight of her and waved. Meg waved back and walked over to say hello. "Trouble with the harness?"

"Oh, you know how old the thing is. Your father can't make up his mind whether or not to sell this buckboard, so he keeps putting off buying a new harness. Right now the last patch job isn't holding."

The sun warmed Meg's back as she glanced at her father. "Parade starts in about twenty minutes, Dad."

"We'll make it." He didn't look up from his repair work. "Nora, can you hold those horses still?"

"If I do, they'll soil this dress, and after all the time I spent making it, I—" Her eyes widened as she looked past Meg. "Why, hello, Luke."

Meg turned, her pulse automatically accelerating. She'd known he was here somewhere but hadn't seen him yet. For the parade he'd chosen a black silk Western shirt tucked into tight black jeans. A black Stetson was pulled low over his eyes. He looked like a devil, and only a devilish urge would have brought him over here to taunt her parents with his presence.

"Hello, Mrs. Hennessy. I'll hold the horses."

Meg's father looked up, his manner painstakingly formal. "Thanks, Luke, but I'm sure you have more important things to do. And you might ruin that fancy outfit."

"Don't worry about it. I have a few minutes. Besides, the parade marshal should be marshaling the parade, don't you think?" He cast a quick smile in Meg's direction and grasped a bridle in each hand. Meg sneaked a peek at her mother. Nora Hennessy's cheeks were bright with color, but Meg couldn't decide if it was from excitement or embarrassment.

The horses, a matched pair of black geldings that were one of her father's few impractical possessions, tossed their heads and shifted restlessly. The harness jingled and Jack Hennessy swore softly under his breath. Luke murmured to the horses and held the bridles firmly. "Nice team," he said to her father.

"Thanks. I should either get them a decent harness or give them up, but I can't seem to do either."

"It's easy to get stuck in your thinking sometimes."

Meg sucked in her breath. Had Luke really said something so pointed? Her father didn't respond, just worked faster. Luke was obviously making him very uncomfortable. He pricked his finger twice. After what seemed like a century to Meg, but was probably only a couple of minutes, her father straightened. "There, that should do it. Appreciate your help." He held out his hand to Luke.

Luke smiled and started to release the bridles, but before he did a camera flashed several times in succession. Meg knew without looking it was that photographer again.

Meg's father let his arm sink to his side. "Guess I should have known it was a photo op, or whatever they call it in Hollywood. In Chandler, we're used to people doing things to be neighborly."

Watching Luke's expression harden, Meg felt her heart break. "Dad! Luke didn't hold those horses for you because he hoped somebody would take a picture.

He's been trying to avoid that woman ever since he got here."

"Never mind, Meg," Luke said gently. "I'd better be going." He pulled fringed black gloves out of his hip pocket. "The parade's about to start."

As he walked away, Meg rounded on her father. "You're being unfair."

"I'm being realistic, Meg. Avoiding cameras? The man's paid to stand in front of one. He offered to hold the horses because he knew the fans would love a picture of him in his black outfit next to those black horses. Even I can see it'll be a great shot."

"You're misjudging him, just like you always have."

Her mother stepped forward. "Now, Meg, this isn't the time to drag all that up."

"I didn't. He did, by being rude to Luke." She glared at her father. "I found out about what happened back in high school, Dad. About how you made Luke break up with me."

Her father met her angry gaze. "I won't apologize for that. Look where you are now. If I hadn't stepped in, no telling what would have happened to you. I guess he told you, huh?"

"Yes. And I was shocked that you'd stoop to blackmail."

"Be shocked, then. Someday if you're a parent, you'll understand what I did. What's he telling you now, for? Does he want to worm his way back into your life?"

"For your information, he told me he understood why you acted the way you did. He's forgiven you, Dad, but you haven't changed, have you?"

"Not when it comes to you. And he's still bad news in my book. I don't care if he ends up with an Academy Award. He's wrong for you. And you know it."

"Your father's right, dear."

Meg turned to her mother. "You're a fine one to talk, considering that you—" She stopped when she saw the anxious expression on her mother's face. Her father didn't know his wife had defected and started watching *Connections*. It was a small thing, but a defection, nevertheless. Meg decided to let the subject drop. "You were right in the first place, Mom. Now isn't the time to be dragging this out." Relief softened her mother's face.

Meg hadn't ever thought much about her parents' relationship, but it seemed strange to her that they would have this sort of secret, no matter how harmless, between them. It made them seem more flawed, less capable of passing judgment on her life. She was both saddened and unburdened by the insight.

"Listen, I have to go. I need to check some last-minute details with Didi." She hurried away.

She found Didi at the registration table set up in a shopping-center parking lot. "Everything looks great," Meg said and gave her a hug.

Didi smiled with pleasure. "Especially our grand marshal. Have you seen the horse they found for him?"

"Horse? I thought a grand marshal rode in the back of a convertibles."

"Luke asked for a horse. Somebody arranged to have an Arabian brought in from a farm in Scottsdale. Luke's right over there. He just mounted up."

Meg looked in the direction Didi was pointing and almost stopped breathing. The horse was black as midnight, with a shimmering mane and a tail that swept the pavement. Sunlight winked on the silver-studded saddle and bridle as Luke guided the prancing animal through the crowd. The yoke of his Western shirt emphasized the breadth of his shoulders, while the black silk revealed the play of muscles beneath it. His black-clad thighs gripped the saddle with practiced ease while his gloved hands firmly controlled the powerful horse. The hat pulled low over his eyes cast his face into mysterious shadow.

"Have you ever seen anything sexier in your life?" Didi whispered.

Meg slowly shook her head. Years ago she'd thought herself a fool to have fallen under Luke Bannister's spell. Maybe now she was a fool for fighting it.

THE REST OF THE DAY passed quickly. Saturday always brought the biggest attendance, and Meg drove her utility cart from one end of the festival grounds to the other, taking care of emergencies. She kept busy until the sun settled below the horizon and the lights of the carnival sparkled against the cinnamon glow of the sunset.

She'd kept her eye out for Clint but hadn't seen him all day. That wasn't surprising. Clint was a party animal who preferred to carouse after dark. But she hoped to find him before he started drinking.

At seven-fifteen she checked backstage at the entertainment pavilion to make sure the country and western group she'd booked was ready to go on at seven-thirty. She was surprised to find Luke there talking with the band members. He excused himself and came over to her. "Can you believe it? They're going to let me play a couple of songs with them. It's a chance of a lifetime, Meg."

She smiled. "What fun. The crowd will love it."

"Come and give me moral support, okay? About eight o'clock."

"I'll try. I haven't found Clint yet."

"He'll show up for this concert, I'll bet. This is one of his favorite groups."

Meg nodded. Clint probably would appear, and he'd see his older brother up on stage, claiming the limelight again. But she couldn't say that to Luke, who looked so excited to have a chance to play with the band. "Good luck with your gig," she said with a grin. "What are you going to play?"

"A couple of easy songs. I told them I was rusty, so they're giving me the simple stuff. I shouldn't screw it up too much."

"You'll be great." Meg knew that all he had to do was stand there with a guitar and the women in the audience would go crazy. "I'll try to be back here by eight."

She kept close track of the time after that. Barring a catastrophe, she'd watch Luke fulfill his dream of playing guitar with a well-known country band. At eight, she arrived at the fringes of the crowd and sat in her utility cart facing the stage.

The crowd was already warmed up by a half hour of their favorite songs before the lead singer announced

Luke Bannister as a guest artist on steel guitar. Wild cheering followed as Luke walked out on stage in his black shirt, tight jeans, cowboy hat and a guitar strapped over his shoulder. When he smiled, the women shrieked, just as Meg had expected they would.

During each number Luke stayed in the background, but for Meg, there was no one else on the stage. She forgot the crowds around her and her responsibilities as festival chairperson. For eight minutes, as the group played two songs and kidded with Luke in between, Meg gave herself up to being a woman in love.

After the second song, amid deafening applause and cries of "More, Luke!" he lifted the guitar strap over his head and leaned the guitar in a corner of the stage. Then he slipped behind the back curtain. Meg watched hopefully in case he came back for an encore, but he didn't. The lead singer started talking about the band's new album, and Meg knew Luke wouldn't return to the stage. She sighed and wished she'd borrowed a video camera for his performance. He was slipping away. Soon he'd be completely gone, and all she'd have would be a well-rehearsed performance on a television screen.

"Did you like it?"

She turned to find him standing beside the utility cart. "I loved it."

"Good. Come down here a sec."

She left her seat and stood beside him. "What?"

"I saw something you should have." He took her hand and led her over to a vendor waving phosphorescent light wands in the air. He bought a multicolored one and fitted the glowing purple, pink and blue rod into a circle. "Hold still." He nestled it on her head like a halo. "There. Perfect."

She gazed up at him with a bemused smile.

He touched her cheek. "You are so beautiful. Dance with me."

"Dance? But—"

"Listen."

She focused on the music coming from the stage, and her hand went to her mouth.

"Just one dance." He slipped his arm beneath her jacket and pressed his palm against the small of her back.

She went into his arms without protest, as the lead singer crooned "You Were Always On My Mind." Ten years slipped away and they were dancing as they had in high school, nestled together, swaying in time to the music, the silk of his shirt making soft shushing sounds whenever she moved.

"Remember?" he whispered into her hair.

"Mmm." She closed her eyes. "We shouldn't be doing this."

"It's our last chance."

"I know." She spoke the words, but they were just words to her. She hadn't allowed herself to focus on his leaving. She hadn't allowed herself to focus on much of anything today. The frantic pace of the festival had kept her occupied, relieving her of the burden of thinking.

Luke brushed her ear with his lips. "I always loved dancing with you. Doing this makes me feel eighteen again."

She sighed and relaxed in his arms. "I'm sorry my father was so rude this morning."

"Don't be. You're not responsible for what he does, Meg."

"If only that photographer hadn't shown up."

"I talked to her today. She's just a kid, really inexperienced. She's got a heck of a name, Ansel Wiggins."

"What did you say to her?"

"She did most of the talking. Wanted to know about you. I said we were old friends, that we'd been brought up like brother and sister."

"Did she buy it?"

"If she didn't, I can't call myself much of an actor, can I?"

Meg knew she should push away from him, but she couldn't force herself to do it. "This isn't exactly the way you'd dance with a sister."

"We're safe for a while. Turns out she loves carnival rides, so I treated her to some tickets earlier tonight, and I didn't tell her about playing with the band. As I said, she's just a kid. She can be handled."

"You asked them to play this song, didn't you?"

"What do you think?"

"I think you're a devil."

He held her tight. "Dancing with an angel. But don't worry. This is just a dance. I'm in control."

That was fortunate, she thought, because she didn't have any when he was holding her like this. She rested her head on his shoulder and wished the song would never end.

Luke's breath fanned her ear and sent shivers down her spine. With each breath she drew in the musky, inviting scent of him. The words of the song tore at her. So what if she was always on Luke's mind, and he on hers? What damn good was that?

The song ended, and Luke slowly released her. "Thank you," he murmured.

She gazed up at him, her eyes filling with tears. "I hate this."

He smiled. "Maybe someday when I'm too old to get good parts and you've served your stint in the White House, we can ignore the world and run away together."

"That's so blasted practical!"

"Want to change your mind about everything?"

She stood there in anguish, wanting to do just that, yet knowing it would be a mistake. "No," she choked out, and whirled away. She ran back to the cart before she started to cry right in the middle of her own festival. She wanted him to follow her, but of course he didn't. She'd made her decision and he was holding back for her sake. There was one thing she could do in return, and she'd do it now. She would find Clint.

Eventually she did, at the shooting gallery with a couple of his drinking buddies. Debbie was nowhere in sight. Apparently Clint was punishing her for Friday night. Meg left her cart and waited while he fired off his allowed shots, missing every one. His friends jeered and clapped him on the back. Clint was reputed to be a good marksman, so obviously she hadn't caught him before he'd started drinking.

As the trio turned away from the booth, Meg called out Clint's name. He squinted in her direction, waved his buddies on toward the beer truck, and swaggered over. "Hi there, Meg. What's up?" He smelled of beer.

"I need a favor."

"Sure."

When he grinned at her, she caught a glimpse of the fun-loving boy he'd been when they were kids. She held on to that memory and tried to forget the beer fumes assaulting her now. "We don't see much of each other these days, Clint."

"Nope." He swayed a little and kept smiling.

"Remember all the good times we had—you, me and Luke?"

His smile faded. "I don't want to talk about him. Can't even watch my favorite group without Luke showing up on the damned stage."

So he had been at the concert. Meg wondered if he'd seen Luke dancing with her. "Luke cares about you, Clint. And he misses you."

"Give me a break. It's all a big publicity stunt. Like everything he does." He started to walk away.

She stepped in front of him. "Wait. Please."

He glanced down at her. "Come on, Meg. Leave me be, okay?"

"Talk to him, Clint. His life hasn't been a bed of roses, either, going out to California alone, making a whole new life for himself."

"I'm crying crocodile tears. Are you through now?"

"No. I promised to deliver a message." She stepped closer and pressed a piece of paper into his hand.

"Here's Luke's room number. He wants you to come over to the San Marcos after the festival tonight, so you two can talk."

"And pose for some nifty publicity pictures? No, thanks."

"Nobody else will be there. You're the only one who will know where he is. It's a chance for the two of you to talk after all these years. Come on, Clint. Luke's the only family you have. Maybe you'll never get along perfectly, but at least give it a try."

"Why should I?"

"Because you need each other, you and Luke."

"He doesn't need anything from me. And I don't want anything from him."

"Go anyway. Please."

Clint looked away from her at the gyrating carnival rides. Then he glanced back at Meg. The drunken haze had left his gray eyes and they'd become brittle. "Sorry, but I don't think I can do that." He turned on his heel and strode off.

Meg's shoulders slumped. There was a slim chance Clint would change his mind. She'd hold on to that hope and not tell Luke just yet that Clint had thrown his offer of friendship back in his face.

THE MORE CLINT THOUGHT about it, the madder he got. He'd been *summoned,* by God. Like some hired hand. Clint pictured Luke relaxing in his suite at the San Marcos, probably with some goddamn silk bathrobe on and a room-service tray at his elbow.

Clint was supposed to go over there and apologize for trying to pick a fight, probably. And then, after Clint begged forgiveness from his majesty, Luke would call in the photographers for a few shots of the two brothers with their arms around each other's shoulders. Fans ate that stuff up.

Clint rode the wildest rides at the carnival with his friends, but he couldn't get rid of the hard knot in his gut. Luke had some nerve. Some damned nerve.

While they were all standing in line for the Whip, he saw that photographer, what was her name? Ansel. How could he forget a name like that? He told his buddies he'd catch up with them later and trotted after her. "Hey, Ansel!"

She turned, took a second to recognize him, and smiled. "Hi, Clint."

"How's it going?"

She shrugged and readjusted her Dodgers cap.

"I take it that means you're striking out."

"I've got lots of pictures, but nothing anybody will pay for, if you know what I mean."

"So you haven't caught him swimming naked in an irrigation ditch or boffing somebody in the back seat of a car?" From what Debbie said, and Clint was inclined to believe her even if he pretended not to, Luke hadn't gotten any sexual exercise on Friday night, at least.

"That's what's so frustrating! My instincts tell me he's involved with the woman who's running the festival, but I can't catch them *doing* anything."

Clint stuck his hands in the back pockets of his jeans. "You think Luke and Meg are getting it on?"

"If they haven't yet, I think they want to. And tonight's the last night he'll be here." She sighed. "So tonight's my last chance to get a worthwhile shot, too. I've spent a lot of money on this trip. I don't think the pictures I have will be good enough to pay my expenses, let alone give me some extra."

Clint turned her theory over in his mind. He'd seen the way Meg had convinced Luke not to fight. He'd seen them dancing after Luke did his sickening bit on stage. Then she'd brought the messsage about Luke wanting to see him. There could be something going on between Meg and Luke. But if Ansel caught them, it wouldn't go so good for Meg. Clint had always liked her.

Except she'd sided with Luke, which come to think of it, she usually had when they were kids. And if she was stupid enough to get mixed up with his brother, then maybe she deserved whatever happened to her.

He dug into his jeans pocket, fished out a crumpled piece of paper and handed it to Ansel. "I don't know if you're right about Luke and Meg, but if you are, this might help you get something juicy."

She held the paper up to the light coming from a concession stand. "What's this?"

"Meg gave it to me. It's Luke's room number at the San Marcos."

9

MEG STAYED UNTIL everything had shut down that night to make sure the trash pickup service had done its job, and the arts and crafts booths and concession stands had been closed and locked up tight.

As she walked to the parking garage where she'd left her car that morning, she thought about Luke and hoped Clint was with him. That hope died when she saw Clint gunning his candy-apple red truck through the exit of the parking garage. She dashed out to the street to see where he was going, but as she feared, he turned left on Arizona and headed away from town. If he'd already gone over to see Luke, the talk hadn't gone well.

But what if he hadn't gone at all? Meg pictured Luke waiting patiently, hoping that, at last, he could forge a link with his troublesome brother. He was counting on Meg to come through for him, and she hadn't done it.

She glanced around the deserted streets. No one would see what she did. She started to head toward the San Marcos. If she met anyone along the way, she could make some excuse about checking a booth or looking for something she'd lost. She wasn't committed to a course of action. Yet.

She passed the dark shapes of carnival rides and the closed flaps of food and crafts booths. A breeze stirred a cardboard cone, which still had bits of cotton candy clinging to it. She picked it up and tossed it into a nearby trash can. No one saw her. No one called out "Still here working, I see."

She crossed Arizona Avenue and glanced to her right at the darkened stage where Luke had performed a few hours ago. The grass had been trampled by thousands of feet, but no one lingered now that the show was over. The beer truck had served its last drink. She turned right, toward the San Marcos.

She'd go in the side entrance, past Cibola, the resort's lounge. If anyone asked, she'd pretend she was going in to have a drink and relax. No one asked. Finding no familiar faces, she kept on walking past Nineteen-Twelve into the patio area.

The pool glowed turquoise in the still night air, and she remembered her halo. She'd kept it on all night, as a private reminder of the dance shared with Luke. She took it off and tucked it into the pocket of her slacks. If she was going to try this crazy stunt, no sense glowing in the dark while attempting it.

She walked under a trellis covered with wisteria vines just beginning to trail their fragrant purple blossoms over the latticework. Pots of petunias hung from the timbers supporting the trellis, and the honeysuckle beside the walkway perfumed the air.

She would only see Luke for a minute, to tell him that Clint hadn't cooperated. Then she'd turn around and go home. Simple as that. The alternative was to leave him waiting for hours for a brother who would never show up.

Meg's heart pounded as she glanced around and crossed to the outside stairway. Who was she kidding? She wanted another chance to be alone with Luke. She could cloak this move on her part with all sorts of noble motives, but the truth was, she couldn't resist the chance of being with him when no one would know.

She climbed to the fourth floor, pausing on each landing to look for observers. There were none. Her mouth grew dry. What was she doing here, risking everything? No, there was nothing to fear, really. Everyone was asleep now. Of course, she knew some of the staff here, but they were all home in bed, not lurking in the halls trying to catch her in some clandestine activity.

She'd stay five minutes, no more. More would be dangerous. She wouldn't let him kiss her, or she'd be lost. Ah, but to be lost with Luke . . .

She approached his room, out of breath from excitement and nervousness. She reached up to rap on the door, put her hand down, took a deep breath, and finally tapped softly. There was no response. She knocked a little louder and looked around, sure someone would appear and ask her what she was doing. No one did. Then the door opened.

Luke gazed at her for a long moment. Then he opened the door wider, and she stepped inside without saying a word. He quickly closed the door and turned the lock.

Her apprehensive gaze took in a cherry dining table, a gray sectional, a round brass coffee table mounded with flowers. And through another door, a bed with a pink comforter and mauve sheets. The bed was turned down.

She faced him and realized she was quivering. He was still wearing his black shirt and jeans, but he'd taken off his boots and unbuttoned his shirt halfway down. She licked her dry lips. "Clint's not—"

"To hell with him." Luke stepped forward and cupped her face in both hands. "Did anyone see you come up here?"

"No."

The lines of concern around his eyes lessened. "Then nobody knows you're here?"

Her heart thundered in her chest. "That's right."

"Oh, Meg." He sighed and caressed her cheeks with his thumbs.

"I just wanted you to know about Clint."

"Thank you."

"I should be going now."

"I don't think so." He leaned toward her, his lips slightly parted.

If I let him kiss me, I'm done for. He held her gently but firmly. One kiss, and then she'd go. This would be the last time she'd ever kiss Luke Bannister. Surely she deserved... Her thoughts ceased as his lips touched hers with a restrained passion that left her shaking.

He lifted his head. "Don't go," he murmured, and kissed her again.

She'd never meant to leave. She knew that now, as she returned his kiss with a fierce joy, opening her mouth to accept what he had to offer, wrapping her arms around his neck and holding on, matching him breath for breath.

He moved from her lips to behind her ear, to her throat. "No one has to know," he murmured. "Surely we deserve this much."

"All I know is how much I need you."

"You have me, Meg." He lifted his head and gazed into her eyes. "You always have. God, but you're beautiful." And with a low groan from deep in his throat, he scooped her up and carried her through the bedroom door and deposited her on her feet next to the bed. Combing his fingers through her hair, he kissed her gently. "But before anything more happens tonight, I want to get something straight."

She could barely think, let alone imagine what he was talking about. "Okay."

He dropped another kiss on her lips before turning and walking into the bathroom. He came back with a fistful of condoms and tossed them onto the bed.

Meg gasped. "You *planned* this?"

"No, I didn't, but I knew that's the conclusion you might make. At my agent's insistence, I bring these along on every trip."

Jealousy surged through her. "Do you...ever use them?"

"Sometimes. When I'm very lonely, and some woman is hooked on Dirk Kennedy. I won't tell you I've never had a one-night stand, because I'd be lying. But it's a joke, really. They go to bed with Dirk Kennedy, and I go to bed with . . ."

She stepped closer, needing to claim her place with him. "Who, Luke?"

He gazed into her eyes. "It's not easy sometimes. Most women wear perfume, and the fantasy keeps slipping away when I smell their skin." He brushed a strand of hair back over her shoulder. "And no one has your exact shade of hair color, or eyes the same vibrant green." He ran his knuckles softly down her throat. "No one else feels quite the same."

"But you make do."

"I'm only human." He pushed her jacket from her shoulders and let it slip to the floor. "Do you know I remember the exact angle of your collarbone? And if someone gave me a piece of clay I could mold the shape of your breast."

"You never should have left!"

"I thought I had to." He tugged her T-shirt out from her slacks, pulled it over her head and let it drop. "Do you know I've never seen you in full light? But I imagine I have." He unhooked her bra and tossed it onto the floor. He was silent for a while as he drank in the sight of her.

Meg lifted her chin. "But you've seen dozens of women like this."

He looked into her eyes. "They weren't you."

"I hate them all."

He stepped forward and drew her into his arms. "Forget them. I'm going to make love to you all night, every minute. We won't sleep. I want to spend every second until dawn holding you, kissing you, moving inside you. Maybe a lifetime isn't in the cards, but we won't think about that, either." He brushed her lips with his. "Let me love you, Meg. I've wanted you for so long."

"And I've wanted you, Luke." She reached for the snaps of his Western shirt and popped them open, the sound as much a celebration as champagne corks bursting from the bottle. "I've dreamed of making love to you from the day I first understood what men and women did behind closed doors. You were the only man I ever wanted."

"That's not true." He unfastened her slacks and pushed them over her hips. "You were married."

"Lord help me, I thought of you every time we made love."

He kissed her hard, so hard she felt the impression of his teeth against her lips. "I hate it that you've been with another man."

"How can you say that?" She ripped at his belt, fumbled with the buttons of his fly. "You've slept with countless women. How do you think I feel when I see you in living color, in bed with somebody else? *That's* why I didn't watch your show, dammit!"

He shucked his jeans, pushed her back onto the bed. "I want to wipe out the memory of anybody else you've been with." He pulled her panties down and threw them to the floor. "I want to love you so hard and so long that you'll never make love again without thinking of me."

She tore at his briefs. "And I want to claim you as no other woman can. They'll never have what I have from you!"

"And no man will know you as I will." He sheathed himself quickly.

"You do that so easily. I hate your having so much practice with other women."

He braced his hands on either side of her head. "There were no other women. Just substitutes for you. Substitutes for this." He pushed forward and gasped. "Oh, God, Meg."

She gazed up at him, his name a sigh on her lips.

His voice was hoarse. "I love you. I've always loved you."

"I've always loved you." She moaned as he thrust again, deeper this time.

"That's it. Cry out. Burn me into your soul. We only have one night."

"No." She dug her nails into his back as he rotated his hips and pressed against the throbbing center of her arousal. "We've had a lifetime. Oh...ohhh!" He moved again, finding the exact spot, honing in on her cries of pleasure, capturing her open mouth with his and mimicking his movements with his tongue.

She'd never been loved like this. Luke knew the flash points of a woman's body the way some men knew the secrets of the internal combustion engine. When she'd nearly reached the point of no return, he withdrew, leaving her gasping. He whispered in her ear, "Not yet." Then he roamed over her breasts with warm, moist kisses and sucked on each nipple until she thought that alone would bring her to climax.

At last he reentered with a rhythm that carried her to the edge. At the crucial moment he slowed his movements. She called out his name in desperate need for fulfillment.

"Easy," he murmured, slowing even more. "Take your time, my love. Now that you're there, make it last." She panted and arched her slick body against his. "Easy." He lowered his head and licked her damp breasts. "You taste like the rim of a margarita glass. Mmm. Like good Russian caviar."

"I'm melting, Luke...melting into you." She felt balanced on a knife-edge, ready to fall at any moment.

"That's what I want. If you wait, if you hold off as long as you can, the end will blow you away."

"It's not fair," she gasped. "You know so much, and I—"

"I've always yearned for you. Wishing someday I could make you feel like this." He eased in and out with the exquisite control of a master.

"Now, Luke, please." Her head thrashed from side to side. "Please."

"Yes." He increased the pace just enough, no more.

She cried out as her body bucked and clenched in a response more powerful than she'd ever known. Wave upon wave of sensation swept over her as he murmured soft encouragement in her ear. The throbbing grew fainter, but before it disappeared he began stroking again. The sensations returned, and she whimpered as he impelled her up, up, back to the pinnacle she'd just left. She clutched his shoulders. "Luke!"

"I love you." He plunged deeper, with an urgency that told her he'd climb the summit with her this time. She lifted her hips to meet each thrust. Her body was a paradox, fluid, yet coiled tight in preparation for the next moment of release.

When that moment arrived, bringing with it a shuddering sweetness that left her trembling, he groaned and buried himself deep within her. She held him fast as convulsions racked him. They lay bathed in moisture and gasping for breath. She caressed his nape, his sweaty back, the firm mound of his buttocks.

He nuzzled her neck and sighed. "Keep touching me, Meg. Don't stop."

"I love touching you. I always have."

"I used to dream about your hands...everywhere...all the places you were too shy to touch when we were dating."

"I used to dream about this . . . you inside me, filling the hollowness, the ache."

"I was so afraid you'd be disappointed."

Her soft laughter shook their joined bodies. "I've never been so undisappointed in my life. I don't even want to think about how you learned to please a woman like that."

"Then don't think about it. Just know that I didn't love them. I love you."

She sighed. "This is so complicated."

"Hush." He nibbled her ear. "Tonight isn't complicated. Don't think beyond tonight. You know what I have in this suite?"

"Lots of condoms."

"Besides that. I have a Roman tub. With jets."

"That sounds interesting."

"It could be. Want some champagne?"

Meg began to feel giddy. "Why not? If this is going to be a night of decadence, we might as well do it right."

"My thoughts exactly. Stay here and fantasize while I find a robe." He disentangled himself from her and levered himself off the bed.

"For me?" she called out after him as he went into the bathroom.

"No, you don't get one. You're not allowed to wear clothes for the next few hours, but somebody has to sign for the champagne."

"Ask for one glass in case they get suspicious."

"I will, but they won't. I'm a crazy actor from Hollywood, right? Did you know they've had people like Clark Gable staying at the San Marcos?"

"Yes. And Errol Flynn and Gloria Swanson. And now you." She heard the squeak of a tap opening and the soft rumble of a tub being filled.

Then he reappeared wearing a terry robe. "I'm not in their league, but all my publicity paints me as a playboy. I could easily have an orgy going on here and no one would be surprised."

"Are you a playboy?"

"No." He walked over and picked up the bedside phone. As he punched in the room-service number, she rolled toward him and loosened the belt on the robe. He glanced down at her, and as she reached beneath the robe to touch him, his lips parted and his eyes closed. He ordered the champagne in a husky voice and slammed the phone into its cradle as he tumbled onto the bed over her. "You witch," he breathed, capturing her hands and holding them over her head. "You wonderful, sexy witch. Don't you realize I have to answer the door in a few minutes?"

"I couldn't help myself."

"And I can't help myself, either." Holding her wrists with one hand, he kneaded her breast and raked her nipple with his teeth.

She writhed against him, unable to believe so much passion existed. He sucked on her breast and stroked his way down across her belly, through the damp hair to the nub of sensation already aching for his touch. She moaned as he rubbed her there. "The tub will overflow."

His breath was hot against her breast. "I don't care." A rap on the door stilled his movements. "But I do want the champagne." He scooped her up. "Kiss me, Meg."

She did, opening her mouth to the hungry thrust of his tongue as he carried her into the bathroom and lowered her into the warm, rushing water. At last he drew back, released her gently and turned off the faucet.

"You've soaked your sleeves."

He shrugged. "I keep telling you, they expect anything from people like me. They're used to wild and crazy celebrities."

"I'm beginning to get used to them, too. At least one of them."

"Be right back."

She slid down, her head propped against the edge of the tub, her body nearly submerged in the jetting water. Every nerve ending was alive and singing. She felt as if she could make love to Luke for days on end and never grow tired of it. He was the only man she'd ever known who could inspire such insatiable desire. No wonder women followed him everywhere. No wonder she'd ended up here tonight, pulled into his arms, into his bed, even into his tub by an irresistible force.

He returned with the bottle of champagne, froth dripping from the neck, and one glass. He poured it full and handed it to her. She raised it in salute and sipped the sparkling gold liquid while her gaze held his. The bubbles coursed through her system, the perfect counterpart to the passions zinging through her body.

Slowly he set the bottle on the edge of the tub and untied his robe. He let it fall to the floor and stood before her, fully aroused. She set the glass beside the champagne bottle and held out her arms. "Come here."

10

LUKE'S GAZE TRAVELED from Meg's flushed face to her rosy breasts cradled by the swirling water. Her nipples beckoned like wine-colored rose petals waiting to be plucked. Her green eyes sparkled with anticipation, and her mouth curved in a smile of welcome. Desire pounded through him.

But he couldn't take her there in the tub. He had to protect her. Already he wanted more than he could have with her. He wanted to throw away the condoms and experience the joy of sliding into her without barriers, the excitement of knowing he could make her pregnant. She was the only woman who made him long for children and permanence.

Foolish thoughts. She wouldn't want children now, maybe not ever, and what kind of father would he make, jetting around the country making appearances?

He wouldn't risk pregnancy tonight. But he could make her cry and moan with pleasure, and that would bring its own kind of satisfaction. He stepped into the frothy water and slid down beside her. She brought the glass of champagne to his lips and he drank. The tart liquid seemed the perfect way to celebrate the realization of a dream. He took another drink, draining the glass.

"More?" she asked.

"Later." He took the glass from her hand and set it on the edge of the tub. Then he drew her forward so her legs rested on top of his and her thighs were open, maddenly close yet not touching his turgid flesh. He positioned her to allow a stream of water from the jets to sluice between her legs. He knew the pulsing water had struck its mark when her breathing quickened and her eyes grew wide.

He smiled. "Nice?" She nodded. With one hand splayed across the small of her back, he reached down and massaged her sensitive spot, adding his touch to the rush of the water. "And that?"

"Yes." She clutched his shoulders and her eyes fluttered closed. He increased the pressure slightly, and she shuddered in reaction, making her breasts quiver. She threw her head back, arched her hips.

He could watch her forever like this, even with the demanding ache in his groin. He would ease that soon. There was still plenty of time. But for now, he concentrated on Meg, his Meg—lost in sensation, immersed in the pleasure he gave her.

She was almost there—he could tell from her quick little gasps, the rocking motion of her hips. He kept on until her gasps became cries and her fingers dug into his shoulders. "Let go," he murmured, pressing harder.

"Luke!" She shook from the force of her release. Then she sucked in great gulps of air. Her face and shoulders were dewy with moisture and the ends of her hair were damp where she'd arched back into the water. Slowly she straightened and focused her gaze on him. "You . . . are a devil."

He smiled.

"I can't believe how you make me feel."

"Tell me."

"Like a courtesan, like someone whose whole life is devoted to physical pleasure."

"That's the way I want you to feel."

"I keep thinking I should be embarrassed because I'm so eager for this. But I'm not."

"Good. Don't be."

Her gaze became dreamy. "And what about you?"

"What about me?"

Beneath the water her hand closed around him. "How do I make you feel?"

His answer was thickened by a fresh onslaught of desire. "As if I could make love to you forever."

"Here in the water?" Her hand glided up and down, and she gazed at him with knowing eyes.

"No." He clenched his teeth as she fondled the sensitive tip.

"Why not?"

"I can't protect you here."

"Surely you know there are ways that don't require protection."

Her hand and the swirling jets were destroying his control. He wasn't sure what she had in mind, but he loved the feral look in her green eyes. She wasn't naive any longer, and he really didn't want her to be. They had no time for games. "I suppose."

She patted the edge of the tub. "Sit here."

"I—"

"Just do it, Luke. Let me make you happy, too." He raised himself to the edge and braced his feet against the bottom. "Perfect." Reaching for the bottle of champagne, she poured more bubbly liquid in the glass. Instead of drinking it, she dipped her finger in and painted a streak of champagne down his throbbing erection. Then, rising to her knees, she licked it away. His senses reeled, and he gripped the edge of the tub. "Nice?"

He nodded. He wanted her to do it again. She did. And again. He trembled.

She took a small sip of the spakling wine without swallowing. Then gently she took him in her mouth. He'd never known such an erotic shock. Cool liquid, fizzing against his skin, and her warm tongue teasing him, coaxing him, driving him closer, ever closer...he couldn't hang on much longer. She took another sip and continued her sweet assault. He groaned. "Meg, I can't..."

She didn't seem to hear him, or didn't care. She was taking control, and he was losing it. Her tongue, her marvelous tongue... He gasped once, and surrendered, the blood roaring in his ears as she took what he could no longer hold back.

When it was over, he sank into the tub and cradled her in his arms. He leaned his forehead against hers and struggled to breath normally. "That...was fantastic."

"I hoped it would be."

"For someone who complained about having no experience, you're very creative. Have you ever—"

"With champagne? Never. But it seemed like a fun idea."

"Oh, it was that." He tilted up her chin and kissed her smiling lips. "And now I think it's time to go back to bed."

"To sleep?"

"Not likely."

He dried her lovingly, and she him. She'd satisfied him completely, yet as he moved the thick beige towel over her body, he felt his craving return. Ten years of wanting had built up a powerful need. He led her to the bed and threw back the comforter. She lay down on the mauve sheets with the sensuous languor of a well-loved woman. God, he treasured seeing her like that.

"The mirrors are a nice touch."

He glanced in the direction of her gaze. She was looking at an entertainment center opposite the bed. He'd paid scant attention to it before, but now he realized that the cabinet's mirrored doors reflected her alabaster body against the dusky mauve sheets. Apparently he'd loved every ounce of bashfulness out of her, because she stretched enticingly and smiled. "This suite seems made for everything we might have in mind."

"It certainly does." He put his knee on the bed and leaned toward her. "Although I'd rather look at you than your reflection." He kissed her mouth, her collarbone, the tip of each breast. She made a soft, feline sound of delight, and when he looked into her eyes, he saw that she was watching him love her. The sight brought a fresh glint of passion to her gaze. "I think I understand the concept of the mirror, now." He trailed kisses over every inch of her smooth skin, careful to pay close attention to the sensitive areas at the crook of her elbows and the back of her knees. She trembled and sighed... and watched all his moves. He grew hard knowing she watched.

With any other woman he would have been self-conscious, but his trust in Meg only heightened his arousal. As she fastened her gaze on him, putting on the condom became an erotic act. When at last he lowered himself deep inside her and they began their special rhythm, she whispered detailed praise of his body in a language that inflamed him even more.

And he realized he wanted the same privilege. Securing her hips tight against his, he rolled onto his back. He looked into her eyes and saw her willingness. Then he gazed past her shoulder and caught his breath at the beauty of her body entwined with his, his hands spread over the seductive curve of her backside.

He touched a small scar there. "Remember?"

She gazed down at him and nodded. "Crawling under the barbed-wire fence trying to get away from a bull."

"I would have fought that bull to keep you safe."

"I know," she said softly. Slowly she began to move, and he was enchanted at the view. Between ragged breaths he told her how much he loved watching her, told her with the same exquisite detail she'd lavished on him. Then passion blurred his vision as together they catapulted over the brink.

Later, as they lay side by side stroking and touching each other as if they'd never have enough, he asked what had happened to the light wand he'd given her before they danced.

"It's in the pocket of my slacks. I took it off when I decided to come up here."

"I want it now." He reached over the side of the bed and searched through their tumbled pile of clothes until he found the glowing circle of light. Then he snapped off the bedside light and unfastened the halo, which became a sinuous strip of color. "I'll never forget dancing with you when you wore this," he murmured, drawing it gently over her body, dappling her skin in pink, blue and violet. "I wanted you so much."

She trembled as he trailed the light wand over her thigh. "And now?"

"I want you even more."

"You're insatiable."

"Do you object?"

"No." She writhed under his touch. "You see, I'm insatiable, too."

With a groan he gathered her close. Tossing the rainbow light to the floor, he began loving her again.

THE CLOCK WAS HER ENEMY. Meg grew angry every time she glanced at its luminous face taunting her from the bedside table. Its bright green hands seemed to spin with breathtaking speed.

She'd never been loved this way, but her precious time with Luke meant more than just enjoying physical passion. They shared quiet times when they talked of their moments together in the past, boisterous times when they laughed and finished the bottle of champagne. She wondered why she wasn't tired at all and gradually realized that love was a far stronger stimulant than caffeine. Love and desperation. She couldn't waste a second in sleep, because these hours might be all she'd ever have. She had to store up enough of Luke to last a lifetime.

She'd decided to leave at four, but as the hour approached she stalled for extra minutes. Reluctantly she began to dress, pausing for kisses, one more caress, his lips on her breasts before she covered them. She had to accept the fact they wouldn't make love one last time, no matter how much she wanted to. Luke pulled on his jeans as if to help her resolution to resist the lure of passion.

She wanted him to ask her to come away with him, yet knew he wouldn't. And deep down, she knew it wouldn't work. She had to stay and he had to go. At last she stood by the door of the suite. "I don't know if I can do this."

"Yes, you can." He gathered her close and kissed her on the forehead. She'd already tucked her halo back into her pocket, although the glow had nearly disappeared.

"I don't know how I can bear seeing you today. I'm afraid I'll give everything away."

"I'll make myself scarce." He cradled her head against his shoulder.

"And the airport." She felt panic rise in her chest. "I was supposed to take you back there tonight."

"I'll get somebody else. Chuck or Didi. Somebody."

"That's good." She was shaking. "I couldn't do it, Luke."

"I know. I probably couldn't get on that plane if you were standing in the terminal."

"Oh, Luke. Why did life have to turn out this way?"

He rubbed the small of her back. "Don't think like that. We had tonight. Some people go their whole lives without a tenth as much."

"That doesn't make me feel any better." She sniffed and wiped her eyes.

"Meg." He held her face in both hands. "Be honest. You may want me, but you don't want my life-style. I'm an actor, not a cotton farmer."

"Maybe . . . maybe I'll give up politics. Maybe—"

"Don't talk like that!" He gripped her more tightly.

"But I love you."

He relaxed his hold and stroked her cheek. "You have a lot more to do in life than love me," he said more tenderly. "So go out and do those things. Be president some day. I'll vote for you."

She gave a watery laugh. "That's a start."

"It's late, Meg." She nodded. "When you leave, go fast. I don't expect anybody will be stirring yet, but if you wait much longer, you might run into an early riser."

"Okay." She lifted a trembling hand to his cheek. "I love you, Luke Bannister."

"And I love you, Meg Hennessy. Now I'm opening this door." He reached for the knob.

She took a deep breath. "Ready." She squeezed his hand and let go as the door opened. Then she hurried through the opening and nearly fell as she tripped over something...someone? There was a cry and Meg stared in horror as a familiar young woman raised her camera. As if in slow motion the camera lens focused on her like the barrel of a gun. *Flash, flash, flash.*

"Meg?"

Numb, she barely heard Luke call out.

The woman scrambled to her feet and backed away, now aiming the camera at Luke, wearing only his black jeans, as he charged forward. *Flash, flash.* Luke swore and grabbed for the camera.

The woman dodged his arm. "Touch me and I'll sue the pants off you!"

"I don't give a damn! Give me that camera." He started forward again.

Meg grabbed his arm and spoke in an urgent whisper. "No. Let her go. Someone will hear us if we don't stop yelling. This could get worse, Luke. Much worse."

A muscle twitched in his jaw. "I'll sue the hotel. They must have told her my room number."

The paparazzo laughed. "That's what you think. I got the number from your brother. Guess he doesn't much care what happens to you."

"My brother?" Luke turned, his expression bleak as he gazed at Meg. "I did this to you. I asked you to give him the room number, and he betrayed me."

She shook her head. "I chose to come up here, Luke. Nobody's responsible but me. If I leave quietly now, maybe this young woman will let me go. She has what she needs, but if we can persuade her to keep her mouth shut, if only for today, the rest of the festival won't be ruined."

"I'm not talking to anybody," the woman said. "In fact, I'm going straight back to L.A. to peddle these pictures. If you get that part you're up for, they'll be worth a lot more."

"You bitch. I'll cancel the screen test."

Meg faced him. "Don't you dare. Maybe I can ride this out. Maybe nobody will want her pictures. They weren't very juicy, anyway. But if you cancel that screen test, Luke Bannister, I will never forgive you. Never."

His chest heaved and his eyes burned with repressed rage. "I guess you'd better get out of here, Meg." He glanced at the photographer. "And that goes double for you."

Meg gave him one last look and started for the stairs. Her heart was pounding and her chest was tight. Okay, maybe it wasn't a complete disaster. Maybe the pictures would never appear in any publication, or if they did, maybe nobody would see them, at least not until after the chamber of commerce election. Maybe, in her haste, the paparazzo had made the wrong settings on her camera.

Meg kept repeating these reassurances to herself as she hurried down the dimly lit stairway. Once she left the hotel she started running. She reached the parking garage out of breath and had trouble putting her key in the lock because she was shaking so much. Not until she was safely home and in her bedroom did she allow the tears to fall.

LUKE WATCHED UNTIL he was certain the photographer hadn't followed Meg. Then he went back inside the room and stood with clenched fists, staring sightlessly at the floor. He'd jeopardized Meg's future. He could never forgive himself for that. He'd give up the screen test in a second if he thought it would do any good, but it would be an empty gesture. Ansel Wiggins would sell her pictures, regardless of whether he became a film star or remained with *Connections*. The only difference would be the price.

He paced the room trying to figure out what had gone wrong. He'd never thought his brother would go this far to hurt him. Obviously he'd misjudged the depth of Clint's anger and jealousy—and immaturity. Giving Wiggins Luke's room number had been vicious and cowardly, but more to the point, childish.

And that in fact was the problem. Clint had never really grown up. What was worse, nobody had ever forced him to. Luke had covered for him back in high school, and the old man had taken over doing it after Luke left. Now, without either of them around, Clint was letting the farm go to hell while he spent a good part of his time soused and joyriding in that shiny red truck.

Luke headed for the bedroom where he grabbed a T-shirt and some boots. This time Clint had gone too far. The joyride was over.

11

LUKE HITCHED A RIDE with a hay-truck driver making an early-morning delivery to a farm near Clint's. He still had to walk about a half mile, and the hike didn't improve his disposition.

The sun had just rimmed the horizon when he reached the Bannister drive. He surveyed the neglect with far less generosity than he had on his earlier visits. The shabby farmhouse surrounded by weeds had ceased being picturesque and now looked shameful. Clint didn't deserve the farm if he couldn't care for it better than this.

Luke went in the kitchen door out of habit. He couldn't remember the last time he'd used the front. The door was unlocked as usual. Luke banged it back on its hinges. "Clint!"

He didn't wait for a response. Maybe Clint was in bed with Debbie Fry. Luke no longer cared. He stormed into the bedroom that had once belonged to his parents.

Clint was alone in the double four-poster. He'd apparently passed out still wearing his T-shirt and jeans. He sat up and rubbed his eyes. "God, my head."

"More than your head is gonna hurt, little brother. Get out of that bed."

Clint peered blearily at Luke. "What in hell —" He paused and then a slow grin spread over his beard-roughened face. "She caught you and Meg, didn't she? I say it serves—"

"Are you going to get out of there, or do I have to drag you out?"

With surprising swiftness, Clint rolled off the bed and landed in a crouch. "Want to get it on, big brother? Or are you still protecting that pretty face of yours?"

Luke faced him, breathing heavily. "I want some answers. What goddamn right did you have to put Meg's career on the line like that?"

Clint moved to the side, positioning himself. "If she went to your room, she did it to herself."

Luke circled in the same direction. They'd choreographed this years ago, in dozens of fights. "Nobody would have known except for you."

"All right." Clint bared his teeth in a sneer. "So I set that up. Small payment, I'd say, for the way you've been setting me up all along."

"Setting you up?" Luke watched Clint's hands, waiting for his first move. "Who took the beatings when something went wrong around here? Who covered for you in that hardware-store deal? Who left without a dime and gave you a clear shot at owning the farm some day?"

"Maybe I don't want the farm!"

"Since the place looks like hell, that's obvious. I'm buying it back."

Clint's bloodshot eyes narrowed. "Like hell you are."

"Why not? Isn't that what you want, a ton of money and no responsibilities? Isn't that what you think I have?"

"I don't think. I know. Prancing around in front of the cameras all day, while I'm breaking my ass—"

"Then give it up, you miserable punk. I could run the place better from L.A. than you can run it living here."

"What a joke. You're a city boy, now. You wouldn't know a boll weevil from a white fly."

Luke flexed his hands. Any minute now Clint would take a swing. He hadn't wanted this fight, but Clint apparently needed it. "I know a son of a bitch when I see one."

The muscles worked in Clint's jaw. "You planning to back that up, or are you gonna refuse to fight, like before? Can't mess up that pretty face, now can we?"

"Try me." Luke licked his lips as they circled.

"Oh, maybe we're serious?" The light of battle gleamed in Clint's eyes. "Well, that's good news. I can hardly wait to beat the shit out of you."

"Same here. You're a sorry excuse for a Bannister." Luke watched the taunts hit the target. "You're a disgrace to the family name. You can't even—"

Clint swung and Luke blocked it neatly. His uppercut caught Clint a glancing blow on the jaw and he staggered. But Clint had been in enough brawls the last few years to have built up his stamina. He came roaring back with a right to the stomach, which Luke dodged, but his left to Luke's chin landed with a solid crack. Luke bit his tongue and tasted blood.

"Better give up," Clint rasped, dancing in front of him. "The next one will break your nose."

Luke swallowed the blood and heaved himself at Clint. They went down, the rag rug by the bed twisting beneath them as they pummeled each other and rolled on the floor. Luke cracked his head on a chair leg, but not before he bloodied Clint's nose. He felt a fierce triumph that he'd drawn blood, even though, in the next second, Clint landed a punch that split his lip.

They grunted and groaned, punched and wrestled, neither getting a clear advantage, neither willing to give up. Luke staggered to his feet and Clint scrambled sideways. Warily he stood and the two began circling again.

"You're weaving," Luke said, steadying himself against a chair. "Give up."

"Not on your life. You're wobbling more than I am." Clint launched another punch and Luke barely sidestepped it. Thrown off balance, Clint slammed into the wall with a solid thud, sending a picture crashing to the floor. He stood still for a moment looking dazed.

Luke shook the sweat from his eyes and tried to catch his breath. "Watch what you're doing."

"*You* watch," Clint panted, "I'm too busy." He lumbered forward, catching Luke in the midsection and sending both of them to the floor again.

Luke tried to push him off but gave up. His arms wouldn't work right. "Get off me, dammit."

"Not now." Clint sprawled over him. "I got the advantage."

With a mighty effort Luke rolled, taking Clint with him. They'd both given up trying to punch each other. Luke now lay on top of Clint, his head spinning.

"Damn," Clint swore, struggling to work his way out from under Luke. "This is hard work."

Luke chuckled. He couldn't help it.

"You laughing or coughing up blood?"

"Both."

"Wanna quit?"

"Do you?"

"Maybe."

Luke rolled over on his back and gazed up at the ceiling. Then he turned his head and looked at Clint. "You're a mess."

Clint returned the look. "You're not too gorgeous yourself. What in hell did you go and do this for? You're gonna be a mass of bruises pretty soon."

"I didn't know any other way to get your attention."

Clint stared at him, and then he looked back up at the ceiling. "You screwed up God knows how many days of shooting that damned soap opera, probably get fined or some such thing, just to get my attention?"

"Worse than that. I have a screen test tomorrow for a movie."

Clint looked at him sharply, and a new emotion flickered in his eyes. "You're an idiot," he said softly. "I'm not worth it."

"I happen to think you are."

Clint closed his eyes. "Damn," he whispered. "Was it . . . bad . . . when Ansel showed up?"

"Wasn't great, but it could have been worse. At least we had most of our clothes on."

"I'll talk to Ansel. Maybe I can buy the pictures from her."

"Too late. She's already on her way back to L.A. She probably had some idea I was a threat to her and that film. Which I was."

Clint's Adam's apple moved. "Well, I sure screwed this up good."

"Yeah. But maybe the damage can be controlled."

"Just tell me what to do."

Luke sat up slowly and winced as he touched his bleeding lip. "Sounds as if maybe you do give a damn."

Clint eased himself up and leaned against the side of the bed. "You, Meg and me go back a long way."

"I got the impression you'd dismissed all that. What changed your mind?"

Clint grinned, but the smile became a grimace when it reached a puffy place on his cheek. "The fact that you were more interested in knocking some sense into me than protecting your face for the cameras. That's the old Luke, the one I remember."

"I've never changed."

"That's not the way I saw it. Ten years ago you washed your hands of me."

"Not you. It was the old man. I got sick of him taking out his frustrations on me, and coddling you."

"Coddling? I worked like a dog around here!"

"All right. Maybe coddling's the wrong word. But he didn't hit you. Maybe to me, at eighteen, that felt like coddling. I hated him and resented you. I got over resenting you, but my stomach still turns over when I think of him."

Clint sighed and leaned his head back against the mattress. "I guess I knew that. I wasn't really surprised when you didn't come to the funeral. I wish you had, though."

"I wish I had, too." He raked back the hair that had fallen over his forehead. "Funny, but I think I could handle that funeral now."

Clint squinted at him. "How come?"

Luke touched his tongue to the cut on his lip. He should probably get some ice, but hell, ice wouldn't fix his face enough for the screen test. So what? "I just think I could, that's all."

Clint studied him for a long while. "It's Meg, isn't it? Getting together with her, I mean."

Luke met his gaze and slowly nodded.

"What now? You moving back here or something?"

"No. I like my job. And I don't want to get in the way of her political ambitions, either."

Clint heaved himself to his feet. "If this is going to be some noble speech about self-sacrifice, I can't face it without a cup of coffee."

Luke laughed and followed him into the kitchen. The back of his head hurt like hell. He felt it gingerly and discovered a nice lump growing there. "Got any ice?"

"Maybe." Clint waved a hand toward the old refrigerator. "Damn thing doesn't always work."

Luke rummaged around in the freezer compartment and found a half-full tray of cubes along with a hoary container of ice cream and a pound of hamburger with freezer burn where the wrapping was torn. He took out the ice tray and ran it under warm water. "This place is a disaster, Clint."

"I know."

"Are times really that tight?" He wrapped some cubes in a dish towel and handed it to his brother. Clint's cheek needed attention as much as Luke's mouth.

Clint plugged in the coffeepot and took the dish towel full of ice. "Yeah, times are tight." He placed the towel against his cheek. "Ow. That smarts."

"You could sell."

"To you?"

"No." Luke pressed his own towel full of cubes to his lip. "I wasn't really serious about that."

"Too bad. What I'd really like is for you to take your half back."

"Why?"

Clint gazed out the grimy kitchen window. "So there'd be somebody else who cared about the place, somebody to talk things over with, help me make decisions."

Luke stood there listening to the coffee perk. He'd thought Clint would be happy to own the farm all by himself. Apparently Luke's gift had been taken as a rejection, a sign that Luke didn't want anything more to do with the farm or Clint.

Clint turned to face Luke. "Okay, lousy suggestion. You don't want to screw around with a farm anymore, and I—"

"No, it's a good suggestion. I'd like my half back. I'd like it a lot."

"Really? You're serious?" Clint's eagerness made him look about seven years old.

"Sure I'm serious. Except we'd have to do most of our business over the phone. I know how you hate all the people I seem to attract these days."

Clint shrugged. "It's no big deal."

"Yeah, but we'd never get anything done."

"I know what." Clint's eyes lit with mischief. "You can come over in disguise. You're an actor, right? Glue on a fake mustache, stick a pillow under your shirt, stuff like that."

"It could work." Luke was miles ahead of him. If he could visit Clint that way, maybe he'd be able to sneak over and see Meg... But no, another backfired plan could wreck her hopes for good. He shouldn't even consider it. And yet... But for now, he had to concentrate on straightening out the problems he and Clint had already made for Meg.

"Then it's settled." Clint stuck out his hand. "You're now the proud co-owner of the Bannister cotton farm."

They shook hands. For a moment their eyes met and they grinned. Then Luke dropped the handshake before either of them got too embarrassed. He glanced around the kitchen. The sink was filled with dirty dishes and beer cans overflowed from the trash. "And the first thing we're going to do as partners is clean this place up. Did you really drink all that beer?"

"I think so."

Luke held his brother's gaze. "Gonna end up like the old man?"

Clint looked away. Then he sighed and ran his fingers through his hair. "I've been thinking about that. Especially after what I said to Debbie Friday night. I never would have insulted her like that if I hadn't been tanked."

"That was my conclusion."

Clint glanced at Luke. "If it's worth anything, I apologized to her yesterday."

"Good."

"But then I got drunk again last night, and hurt you and Meg."

Luke couldn't let him off the hook. "That's right."

"So I guess it's time to lay off the booze for a while."

"Yep."

Clint nodded. "It was losing its appeal, anyway." He was quiet for a few moments, and then he tossed his dish towel full of ice in the sink. "How about some breakfast? I'm a damned good cook."

"I'm glad one of us is," Luke said. He felt as if a weight had been lifted from his shoulders. Underneath his party-boy exterior, Clint had a strong will. If he'd decided to give up drinking, he'd do it, and probably without a lot of fanfare. "I'll pour us some coffee," Luke offered. "And while we're eating and cleaning up the kitchen we'll figure out how to help Meg."

"Yeah. We got her into this, so it's up to us to get her out."

"Just like in the old days."

Clint smiled. "Just like in the old days."

AFTER DRIPPING SOME Murine in her eyes, downing two cups of coffee and putting Dog-breath in his run, Meg headed for the ostrich festival at nine. The festival opened at ten, and the chairperson needed to be there early. She didn't want to go—in fact, she would rather clean the floors of the livestock trucks with a toothbrush, but she had to see the day through and somehow pretend everything was fine. If she kept away from Didi, she might succeed in fooling everyone else.

Sure enough, Didi's was the first call that came from Meg's walkie-talkie after she arrived. The box of extra festival programs had disappeared. Meg had no choice but to drive her utility cart over to the information booth and find out what had happened to the blasted programs. On the way over she decided to keep her sunglasses on at all costs.

She drove up to the information booth where she found Didi rummaging through boxes looking for the brochures. "Good morning," she called, hopping down from the cart and giving Didi a big smile.

Didi glanced up, stared at Meg and got up from the box she'd been searching through. "Okay. What's wrong?"

"Why, nothing." Meg held onto her smile with great effort. "Have you tried that green box over there? I think the last time I saw the brochures, they were in—"

"You look like hell."

Meg glanced down at her T-shirt and jeans. "It's the same outfit you have on."

"Not your outfit, your face. Your posture. You look like somebody died."

Meg glanced away and swallowed. "I was hoping nobody could tell."

"Tell what?" Didi frowned. "Oh, God." She pushed through an opening between two tables and hopped into the driver's seat of Meg's utility cart. "Get in." Meg obeyed and Didi drove the cart to a secluded area behind the entertainment pavilion. "Okay. What happened?"

Meg took off her sunglasses and wiped her eyes. "The worst." She told Didi the whole story, only omitting the intimate details of her passionate night with Luke, but leaving no doubt as to what had happened between them. When she finished describing the disastrous ending, Didi put her arms around her while she cried.

"Don't blame yourself," Didi murmured. "I doubt any normal woman in your circumstances would have done any different. And no one would ever know, except for that snake in the grass Clint Bannister. I could wring his neck, not to mention performing a few other alterations to his anatomy."

Meg sniffed and blew her nose on the tissue Didi gave her. "If this gets out, I can kiss that chamber presidency goodbye. And my plans to run for the legislature."

"Maybe it won't get out."

Meg shook her head. "You know how these things go, Didi. They *always* come out, and usually at the worst possible time. I have no doubt that woman will sell her pictures to someone. If Luke gets the part he wants, the pictures will get more play than ever. My only hope is that they don't appear where Chandler people can see them until after the chamber election." She sniffed again. "Of course I could be thrown out after I'm elected. That would be even worse. Maybe I should just drop out of the running."

"You most certainly should not. We need you in that job and we can't let one little thing—"

"One big thing, Didi."

"All right, one *big* thing stop you. Now, my first bit of advice is to announce you're plagued by allergies, so people will have an explanation for your appearance."

"But I've never had allergies."

"You do now. Came on just like that." Didi snapped her fingers. "It can happen. Second thing is, talk to Luke before he leaves and find out if he can do anything to supress those pictures. I'm sure he has some contacts in L.A. and even in New York. Maybe if he agrees to do an exclusive interview, or pose as a centerfold for somebody—"

"Didi! I couldn't ask him to do that."

"Then I will."

"No! I'll talk to him. I promise." Meg's pulse raced in alarm at the thought of dealing with Luke again, but Didi was right. Maybe Luke could do something, something honorable of course, in exchange for the pictures.

"Okay. And number three, except for that brief conversation, and I emphasize brief, keep away from Luke Bannister. Unless, of course, you want to change the whole course of your life?" She glanced at Meg with eyebrows raised.

Meg stared down at her hands twisted together in her lap. "No."

"I wouldn't blame you if you did."

"I've thought about it a hundred times since I left him this morning, and always come to the same conclusion. I've been fascinated with politics ever since I was president of our Girl Scout troop. This is my shot, Didi, and I'd never forgive myself if I threw it away."

"Then you can't."

"Besides, Luke would lose respect for me if I ran away with him. One of the things he loves about me is my commitment to causes I believe in. He admires me for going into politics." Meg gazed at Didi. "I wouldn't be the person he loves if I gave all that up."

"What about him? Would he come back here?"

Meg shook her head. "And I wouldn't want him to. He's so exciting the way he is, Didi. It would be a crime to try to turn him back into a Chandler farm boy."

"I agree." Didi sighed. "Well, ready, kid?"

"Sure."

Didi started the utility cart. "You can help me find those damned brochures, and I think Luke's making one last appearance with the festival mascot at ten. You can go over to the petting zoo then."

"Right."

12

AT A LITTLE PAST TEN Meg drove the cart over to the petting zoo. For the past few minutes, she'd taken deep breaths and tried to stay calm, but nothing seemed to work. How could she stay calm when she was about to come face-to-face with a man she'd loved intimately hours before and would probably never see again after today?

As she neared the petting zoo, Luke was signing autographs. His back was to her, so she slowed the vehicle and allowed herself to adjust to seeing him again. He wore a tan cowboy hat, a white Western shirt and a pair of tight blue jeans. Her eyes burned with unshed tears as she watched him lean toward a little girl and return her stuffed autograph hound. Luke had always been good with kids. She'd forgotten that. Once, a long time ago, she'd dreamed of having Luke's children.

The little girl pointed toward Luke's face and asked a question Meg couldn't hear. Luke laughed and said something that made the girl smile. She left with her parents, and Meg decided to grab her opportunity. She hopped out of the cart and walked quickly over to him.

When he turned in her direction, she gasped. His lower lip was swollen and cracked. His right eye was half-closed and puffy, with bruises underneath, and there was a long scratch across his cheek. "Luke! What on earth—"

He smiled as best he could. "You should see the other guy."

"You had a fight with Clint, didn't you?"

Just then, Clint walked up, a cup of cola in each hand. "The truth is, *I* fought him. And I won." He handed one cola to Luke and offered the second to Meg. "Want this?"

"No...thanks." She stared at the two brothers. They acted as if they were the best of friends.

"Then I'll drink it. Or hold it against my cheek for a while. That feels good, too."

"I don't know which of you looks worse."

They both spoke at once. "He does," they said, pointing at each other. Then they began to laugh, but the laughs soon turned to groans of pain.

Meg was totally bewildered. she'd never understand men. "Well, I hope you're both really proud of yourselves. Especially you, Luke. What about your screen test tomorrow?"

"Maybe they'll let me read the fight scene, or I should say, the scene after the fight scene."

"You don't seem very upset about it." She was impatient with his attitude. Didn't he understand what he'd done to himself?

"I'm not upset."

"He's not upset," Clint said, jerking his thumb at Luke. "By the way, you should be nicer to him, Meg. He busted his face for you." Clint chuckled until the laughter hurt too much and he stopped.

Meg glared at them. "I hope that's not true."

"Nah, it's not." Luke sipped his cola and winked with his one good eye. "It just made me feel better."

"That's great. Just great. And I thought you two had grown up. What sort of example are you setting?"

Luke glanced at Clint. "Does this sound like a familiar speech to you?"

"Seems I've heard those words a few times. And she always tilts her chin up that way when she's giving us a lecture about our behavior."

"It's kind of cute, don't you think?" Luke's good eye twinkled.

Meg clenched her fists. "Luke Bannister, you are the most maddening—"

"It'll be okay, Meg. Don't worry. They can reschedule the screen test if they really want me, and makeup can do wonders."

The underlying softness in his voice was nearly her undoing. She swallowed. "I hope you're right."

"I'll be fine."

She stood there trying to remember what message she'd been sent to deliver. Oh, yes. The photographer. "Listen, I, uh, talked to Didi."

He raised an eyebrow.

"She made me promise to ask. Is there any chance you can talk the photographer out of publishing those pictures?"

"I plan to try."

Clint stepped closer and lowered his voice. "And if that doesn't work, and they come out, I've got a friend who distributes those magazines and tabloids around to the stores. I think I can delay the pictures hitting the stands until after the election."

"And then they'll throw me out of office."

Luke shook his head. "I don't think so, Meg. You have a lot of support in town."

"Hey." Clint put his arm around her shoulders and shook her gently. "Don't worry. Luke and I will come through. Remember the bull? Didn't we save you from that stampeding bull?"

Meg glanced at Luke and blushed. "I guess so." His gaze was steady, and she knew he wasn't remembering the day they'd run from the bull, but the passion of their early-morning lovemaking, when he'd rediscovered her scar.

"The only problem you had was sticking your fanny in the air when you crawled under the barbed wire," Clint said. "Any idiot knows not to do that."

"I wouldn't call her an idiot," Luke said. "What about that day you tried to build a fire with cow chips, pretending they were buffalo chips?"

"How would I know they'd stink like that?"

Meg smiled. "And then we couldn't put it out. The water made it steam like crazy, remember?"

Clint held his bruised cheek while he laughed. "Like a hundred cows passing gas."

"Yeah," Luke said. "Then we had to cart the whole mess off in our wagons. Never did get those wagons to smell good again."

"I tried to paint mine," Meg said. "Ugh."

"And remember the time we found that half-dead chicken, and—" Luke paused as two teenagers came up to him for autographs.

Meg edged away. "Maybe I'd better go."

"Wait a sec." He signed the autographs and posed for pictures, kneeling down with a girl on each side and the baby ostrich in the background. Clint offered to operate the girls' camera.

"What happened to your faces?" one of the girls asked.

"One of those revolving doors," Luke said. "He was coming in and I was going out."

"Yeah," Clint added, "a killer revolving door. Watch out for them. They just keep coming at you."

The girls looked at each other, giggled and ran away.

"You two are a pair," Meg said. And they were a pair, she thought. Whatever else would come of this, Luke and Clint were back to being brothers again. In a twisted sort of way, she'd brought it about, just like when they were all kids together. From the corner of her eye she saw another group of autograph seekers approaching. And she couldn't stand here forever. People might talk. "I really have to go."

Luke grew very quiet. "I'll call."

Her heart wrenched. "Maybe . . . that's not such a good idea. I don't think talking on the telephone would . . . I mean, it's not . . ."

Clint turned his back on them and professed great interest in the baby ostrich.

"You're right," Luke said softly. "Bad idea."

"But I would like to know if you get the part."

"I'll let you know through Clint. He'll tell you if I get it."

"Okay."

"Say goodbye to Dog-breath for me."

"I will."

"Take care."

"You, too." She gazed at him until tears blurred her vision. She turned quickly and hurried away without looking back.

ENDURING THE DAY until four, when Luke was scheduled to leave, was an experience Meg hoped never to repeat. His presence dangled temptingly in front of her and several times during the day she had to remind herself of the reasons why she couldn't get on the plane with him. Whenever the tears came, she used Didi's allergy story as an excuse if anyone caught her with red eyes and a sniffly nose.

Then, at last, he was gone. The festival continued with ostriches racing, music blaring and vendors aggressively marketing their wares for the last two hours available to them, but for Meg the grounds seemed empty and lifeless. A wave of fatigue overcame her now that Luke was gone. Fortunately everyone expected her to be exhausted, and they made jokes and patted her on the back. Congratulations came from all sides on the success of the festival. The best ever, many said. Even the Bannister boys fighting and making up again added to the fun, some commented. She began to wonder if she'd imagined her night with Luke.

Then, as if to confirm she hadn't, Didi came along, looked deep into her eyes and gave her a big hug. "You'll survive this," she murmured.

Meg wasn't so certain.

WITH DIDI'S HELP, Meg got through the next two weeks. Didi was taking over as festival chairperson the following year, so Meg spent long hours with her making the transition. Meg was glad to have the work, and especially grateful to be doing it with Didi, who understood her mental lapses and emotional outbursts. Meg used much of her spare time helping get the books in order for her computer consulting firm.

Evenings were tough. She took Dog-breath for long walks to tire herself out so she'd sleep at night. The walks helped, and she savored the scent of citrus blooms that filled the air, the gentle warmth of the air and the rising moon. Nevertheless, her unhappiness persisted. Sometimes Meg would sit down in a grassy field sprinkled with wildflowers, hold Dog-breath close and cry into his soft coat. He'd endure stoically and lick her face before they made the long trek back home.

Although it was like flaying herself, she still tuned in *Connections* every weekday. Watching Luke on screen made her ache with longing. She'd tried to break herself of the habit, but with no success so far. Apparently Luke hadn't gotten the part in the movie. Clint hadn't called with any news, and she wasn't about to call him. At least not yet. She should have asked him to let her know one way or the other, but it was a wonder she'd had any coherent thoughts the day Luke left.

She hadn't spoken to her parents since the festival. When her mother called and invited her to dinner, Meg reluctantly accepted, and suffered through the meal making small talk about the cotton crop while worrying about what would happen if the paparazzi's photos appeared on the newsstands in Chandler. Unfortunately her parents would share in her disgrace. And they'd warned her to stay away from Luke.

Over cherry cobbler dessert, her father cleared his throat, usually the signal that a pronouncement was coming. Meg waited, her heart pounding in her ears. Maybe he'd heard about the incident already.

"Talked to Clint the other day," her father said. "It seems Luke's taken back half ownership of the farm."

Meg blinked. She was unprepared for the rush of hope the news brought. "You mean he might be spending time here?"

Jack Hennessy glanced sharply at his daughter. "That isn't Clint's understanding. The idea is that now Clint will have somebody to talk over plans and problems with. Luke will be more of a silent partner. I think Clint needs that. He's pretty young to have sole responsibility for that farm."

"I suppose." Meg tried to hide her disappointment. Of course Luke wouldn't be reestablishing himself in Chandler. He'd made that clear before.

"Anyway, after hearing that, I think I might have misjudged Luke, and I wanted to tell you so. He behaved himself while he was here. Even that fight with Clint turned out to be a good thing. Clint mowed the weeds and the painters are out there now. I figure that's Luke's influence."

Meg gazed at her father. He didn't know the half of Luke's influence, or whether Luke had "behaved himself," but she wasn't about to snatch defeat from the jaws of victory. "Too bad you can't say that to Luke himself."

"Well, I will, if I ever get a chance, although I probably won't. When would I ever have reason to be around a big Hollywood star?" He rested his arm on the table. "Now don't get me wrong. I maintain my position about you and Luke. He's wrong for you. Always was, always will be. I . . . uh . . . understand you know about the deal in high school."

"I know, and I don't like it." Meg was still angry about what her father had done ten years ago, but her worry about the revealing photos of her and Luke took precedence over her anger.

"You don't have to like what I did. I didn't do it to win a popularity contest."

"Jack, now let's not spoil the mood with this kind of talk. You wanted Meg to come over so you could tell her about Luke taking back half of the farm. Let's not get into that other business. It's over with, anyway."

Jack Hennessy frowned and rustled his napkin as he shoved it under the edge of his plate. "I didn't want her here just to talk about Luke, Nora. It was time we had Meg over to catch up on how she's coming along."

"That's true." Her mother smiled nervously. "We're so proud of how you handled the festival. Everyone is raving about how good it was this year. And now you'll certainly be elected president of the chamber. Just think."

"She's achieving her goals, that's what she's doing," her father said, his voice gruff. "She's not allowing herself to be sidetracked. With an attitude like that, you can have anything you want, Meg."

Meg fought the urge to tell them about Luke and about the pictures, just to get the agony over with. But her parents had always counseled her not to buy trouble. Maybe Luke could convince the photographer not to sell them. Maybe he already had.

HENRY DAVIS RANTED and raved about Luke's bruises, but eventually he got on the phone, called in some favors and had the screen test postponed. The shooting of *Connections* for the next week was no big deal—the writers enjoyed the challenge of explaining his battered face as part of the story line.

And finally Luke asked Henry to help him track down Ansel Wiggins. Fortunately Henry knew almost everyone in town, and within twenty-four hours he had a phone number for Ansel Wiggins, photojournalist. Luke called the number during a break on the set.

The answering-machine message began with the screeches and trumpeting of jungle animals. Then Ansel said, "Ansel Wiggins is covering an African safari with Prince Charles. Her assistant will forward your message. Please leave your name, number and position on the food chain after the beep."

Luke grimaced. He wasn't crazy about leaving his home number. She might sell that, too. But he did it, anyway.

When she hadn't returned his call two days later, he tried her number again. The message had changed. This one began with flute music and the howl of a wolf. "Ansel Wiggins is covering ancient Native American ceremonials with Shirley MacLaine. Please leave your name, number and astrological sign after the beep."

Luke left both his studio and home numbers and told Ansel that the call was urgent. He decided to give her another day before he tracked her down in person. She called at midnight, waking him up. "I'm sorry. I'm a night person and I didn't think about the time," she explained.

Luke shook off the fog of sleep. "Can we meet for coffee?"

"Sure. How about now?"

He groaned and glanced at the clock. He was due on the set in seven hours, but this elusive woman had to be dealt with, and fast. "Okay. Now."

Half an hour later he walked into the all-night coffee shop she'd agreed upon. She was tucked into a booth, chewing gum and studying the menu, still wearing the backward baseball cap, sloppy T-shirt and oversize shorts. The only difference in her appearance was the lack of cameras. Luke sighed and headed over.

She glanced up. "I'm having a triple hot-fudge sundae. How about you?"

"Just coffee." He sat opposite her. "I want to apologize if I was rough on you the other morning, but that woman is a close friend of mine."

She folded her arms and leaned on the table. "So I gathered."

She had a smart mouth. He steeled himself to ignore her or they'd be shouting at each other before long. He took a deep breath. "I'll make this short—" he paused as the waitress arrived and took their order "—I want the pictures, negatives, too. I'm prepared to pay for them."

"I'll bet you are." She popped her gum. "What happened to your face?"

"Never mind that. Name your price."

"Can't."

"Why not?"

She gazed at him. "Because somebody else already bought them. I got the money up front, and if you land the movie contract you're trying for, I get a bonus."

"Dammit! Don't you realize you could ruin a potential political career? You look like a feminist. Don't you want a woman in a position of power?"

"Yeah, I do. Me. And I finally made it." Her order arrived. She parked her gum on a napkin and ate the cherry off the top of her sundae.

"But you made it at the expense of someone else."

"Now just a minute, Luke Bannister. If you get that movie part, won't that be at the expense of someone else?" She waved her spoon at him. "I'm sure you're not the only actor in town who'd like to star in that film."

"But it's not the end of a career to lose one part."

"How do you know that? How do you know if this is not the last chance before that person packs up and leaves town? How do you know whether the guys trying for this part are down to their last nickel and another rejection means going home to sell used cars in Topeka? You know as well as I do what the world is like. Your friend might as well know it, too." She dug into her sundae and rolled her eyes at the first gooey bite.

Luke's stomach knotted as he realized how helpless he was to stop the publication of her photographs. No matter how right Ansel was about the ways of the world, he didn't want Meg buffeted by the same winds that had pounded at him for most of his life. But he could take it, was used to it. She wasn't. "Where did you sell the photos?"

She was proud enough of her sale to tell him, with her mouth full of ice cream. He winced. The New York-based tabloid had a wide circulation. Tossing some money on the table, he left his coffee sitting there and walked out of the restaurant. He had some thinking to do. The tabloid wouldn't squelch the photos. They'd run them, even if he didn't get the part. Meg was in trouble.

13

ON THE EVENING OF April first someone knocked at Meg's front door. She glanced down at her cotton blouse, the shirttails hanging out over a worn pair of plaid shorts, and her bare feet. If this was chamber business, she wasn't dressed for it.

Dog-breath ran ahead of her as she went to answer the door. She looked through the peephole and saw an overweight man with a beard, thick glasses and a feed-store cap. He was dressed in a flannel shirt and baggy jeans, and carried a thick catalog under one arm. A blue Geo sedan was parked in the drive.

"He's selling something," she muttered to Dog-breath. Taking a firm grip of the dog's collar, she opened the door a crack. "Yes?"

"Your neighbor Clint Bannister sent me, ma'am." His voice was reedy and rather unpleasant. "Said you might be interested in looking at some seed catalogs."

Meg sighed. "I'm sorry, but I don't have time to put in a garden this year. Besides, it's a little late in the spring for seeds."

"I can have bedding plants shipped, too."

"I—hush, Dog-breath." She glanced down in surprise at the retriever, who was whining and wagging his tail. She'd always considered him a good watchdog, but now she was having her doubts.

"Then maybe I could trouble you for a glass of water, ma'am."

"Excuse me a minute." Leaving Dog-breath to guard the door, she walked back to the kitchen to call Clint and verify that this guy was legit. Clint confirmed that he was and suggested she order something from him.

Meg returned to the door, still debating whether to do that or not. She knew the old glass-of-water ploy. Once inside the door the guy would convince her to look at his stupid catalogs. Then again, maybe she should plant a few vegetables. At any rate she was glad Clint had ordered some; it was a sign that he was getting his life back together.

The man looked kind of pathetic standing there, and Meg relented. "All right. I'll get you a drink." She opened the door. "If you'll sit down, I'll be right back with the water." She closed the door and started toward the kitchen. Looking back over her shoulder, she noticed Dog-breath licking the man's hand. What had gotten into that mutt?

When she returned with the water, the man was leaning back against the cushions of her sofa and making himself at home, although he still hadn't taken off his cap. Meg regretted her softheartedness already. The guy would probably stay forever. Apparently Dog-breath had taken leave of his senses, because he'd laid his head on this stranger's knee. "Your water."

He took the glass and set it on her coffee table without drinking it. Then he gazed at her.

"I'm really not interested in a garden this year," she said. "So if you'll drink your water, I have some other things to do this evening."

"Then maybe I can interest you in a new product that takes care of jock itch."

She stepped back, startled. Her heart began to pound as she looked more closely at the man. The lenses of his glasses were very thick, and his eyes were brown. He reached out to stroke Dog-breath's head and she looked at his hand, then back at his face. She gasped.

He took off his glasses, then his cap. He popped out the brown contacts and put them on the table. Last of all he peeled off the beard and tossed it onto the coffee table next to the untouched glass of water.

"My God!"

He stood and grinned in triumph. "April Fools! I thought if you didn't know me, no one would."

"Luke!" She hurled herself at him and he caught her in his arms.

His lips found hers, but he groaned in frustration as the padding under his shirt wedged them apart. "I've put on a little weight and I can tell it's going to come between us."

"What about your movie deal? What about your screen test? Did you—"

He cradled her face in his hands. "Dirk Kennedy is dead. Shooting starts next week for *The Unvanquished*. The only problem is—"

"Then you got the part?"

"Yes, but I'm afraid it will—"

"Luke, that's wonderful." She gave him a long, lingering kiss. "Tell me about the movie."

"It's a historical romance set in the eighteen hundreds, based on a book by Helen Goodwin. I get a young girl pregnant and then I'm captured by Indians before I can make an honest woman of her. I escape from the Indians just in time to save her and the baby from a raid."

"Sounds steamy." She began unfastening the buttons of his shirt. "Speaking of which, isn't this flannel hot?"

His eyes darkened with passion. "Oh, Meg, I hope you know what you're doing."

"Inviting a door-to-door salesman into my bed. And don't tell me you don't want to be there."

"More than you know."

"Then come with me." Without another word, she led him to her bedroom and closed the door.

Leaning against it, she held his gaze as he finished unbuttoning his shirt. She remembered the last time he'd undressed in her presence. And all that had followed. An insistent ache invaded her loins.

Maybe she was just setting herself up for more heartbreak. But he was here, and in the bedroom where she'd fantasized about him every night for two weeks. She couldn't send him away. Not yet.

He pulled the padding out of his shirt and tossed it aside. The jeans, way too large now, rode low on his hips. She walked toward him and caressed his bare chest, stroking her fingers through the thick mat of hair.

"Oh, Meg. I've missed you so much." He undid the buttons of her shirt.

"I've missed you." She kissed the hollow of his throat as he pushed the blouse off her shoulders. "I never thought I'd be able to touch you like this again." She felt his heart pounding rapidly against her palm. She leaned down and flicked her tongue over his nipple until it hardened in response.

He fumbled with the back hook of her bra before he finally got it undone. "I want you too much. I'm shaking."

She stood on tiptoe. "Kiss me, Luke. Kiss me hard." His mouth ground against hers with a sweet pain that she welcomed because it made his being there with her real. She kissed him back, teasing his tongue with hers, plowing furrows through his hair with her fingers.

With one hand he stripped away her shorts and panties before carrying her to the bed. He tumbled with her onto the comforter, kicking off his shoes as he kissed her shoulders, her throat, her breasts. "I've missed you, missed you, missed you," he chanted, running his hands over her body until she writhed against him and tugged at the waistband of his jeans.

He unfastened them quickly and shucked his briefs. She filled her hand with him and he groaned with pleasure as she squeezed and stroked. At last he stilled her hand and reached over the side of the bed, searching in his jeans pocket. In a moment he was back, and she helped him ease the condom on, placing kisses along the way.

"I wanted to take this slower," he gasped, moving between her legs. "But I can't, Meg."

"Love me," she begged, pulling him down, pulling him into the center of her being.

His movements were basic, elemental. She rose to meet each powerful thrust with a deep need of her own. Now was not the time for flourishes. They strove to reconnect, to drive their love into each other's body with a force that would never shake it loose. Their climaxes came quickly, and they clung together through the ebbing waves of passion.

Finally they lay quiet, breathing in the same rhythm, listening to each other's heartbeat. Luke propped himself up on one elbow and gazed into her face. He smiled, but his eyes were shadowed.

"What is it, Luke? You were trying to tell me something before, but all I could think about was your movie."

"And this?"

"Oh, yes."

He kissed her gently and drew back. "It's not right that something as wonderful as this can end up hurting you."

Then she knew. "You can't stop the publication of the pictures."

He shook his head. "I've talked to some people in New York, and it doesn't look good. When they learn I've signed to do this film, they'll give the pictures even bigger play."

Meg swallowed. "I guess that's show biz."

"When's the chamber meeting where you'll be elected?"

"The third Wednesday of this month."

"I'll think of something to stall them."

"Remember, there's Clint's friend, the one who knows when the tabloids are delivered to the stores."

"Clint's already talked to him. He's an old drinking buddy, so he'll do what he can, as long as we don't ask him to put his job on the line." He caressed her cheek with his thumb. "I hate how the whole thing has turned out for you."

"I don't. I'll weather it. And I don't regret a minute we've spent together, Luke."

"I can't regret it, either. I probably should, considering how it's affected you, but I can't. Even coming here tonight was a silly risk, but I had to see you."

"I'm glad you did. How long can you stay?"

"I'm leaving tomorrow. I spent the afternoon at the house with Clint."

She refused to let sadness overwhelm her at the thought of him leaving so soon. "And the night belongs to me."

"I belong to you."

Meg circled his ear with the tip of her finger. "So Dirk is really gone?"

"Yep. Piloted a plane over the Bermuda Triangle to prove it was no big deal. He was never heard from again."

"Sheila will miss him."

"Mmm."

"You sure look convincing in bed with her." Meg didn't tell him of the jealousy that knifed through her every time he touched the actress. "You're all sweaty and flushed, just—"

"Like this?" He nuzzled the side of her neck.

"Yes."

"It isn't anything like this."

"You could have fooled me."

Luke chuckled and pushed himself away from her. "I'll be right back, and then I'll show you just how it's done—on the set." He returned from the bathroom and put on his French-cut briefs. "First of all, I wear something like this."

"That's a relief." She viewed the bulge of masculinity revealed by the skimpy navy briefs. "Sort of. And what does Sheila wear?"

"A bodysuit. It looks like she has nothing on, but she's covered everywhere important. It's all camera angles."

"If you say so."

"Okay, we'll imagine you're in the bodysuit. I lie down and arrange myself so I'm partially covering you, and the comforter hides the rest, but we reveal just a little skin here, and here." He lay across her with his weight on his elbows. "Push your breasts up a little. That's it. Very nice."

"How do you feel when you're on top of Sheila like this?"

"I'm thinking about my lines."

"Sure you are."

He grinned at her. "Okay, most guys aren't going to gripe about holding a woman with a nice body, but let me tell you the downside. If you were Sheila, you'd have on a ton of makeup."

"Want me to put some on?" She started to get up.

"No." He held her close. "We're simulating here. Also, you'd have your hair in a certain arrangement, with hair spray and stuff on it. It wouldn't feel like yours does." He ran his fingers through her hair. "I love your hair."

"You're digressing."

"Okay, so here we are, makeup and hair spray, and people all around us. Hot lights. Cameras moving in. This is not an intimate experience. Then somebody mists us with a spray bottle."

Meg laughed. "They spray you with water?"

"That's how we look all sweaty and flushed, like we're really worked up." He ran a finger down the side of her cheek. "Fortunately you have the genuine thing, so we'll skip the spray bottle."

"What happens next?"

"I look into your eyes, and I say my line."

"Say one. Be Dirk Kennedy."

"Okay." He cleared his throat, and glanced away from her for a moment.

She watched in fascination as his features hardened just a little. When his gaze returned to hers, it glittered with a quality she'd never seen in Luke, and she was reminded that Dirk Kennedy wasn't a very nice guy. His voice was tight, almost ferocious. "You lured me to your bed, Sheila. Don't think you can tell me to stop now."

A shiver slid down Meg's spine. "I don't want you to stop."

Luke's mouth came closer; his breath fanned warm air across her face. "I think you want your husband to find out about us."

"No! I swear!"

"I've heard you taunt him." He hovered over her lips. "Just as you taunt me."

"No," she whispered, wanting his kiss, no matter who he was pretending to be.

"Yes, and you'll pay for your taunts, my love." He kissed her almost brutally while he reached for her uncovered thigh and raked his spread fingers down it.

Meg responded to his kiss, opening her mouth and arching her back, crushing her breasts against his chest. Luke plunged his tongue into her mouth and rotated his hips against hers. She pressed upward against his arousal and whimpered at the barrier of cotton between them.

He lifted his mouth from hers a fraction. "Do you want me?"

"Yes!"

"Then beg me, you witch."

"Please, Dirk . . . oh, please."

He chuckled low in his throat and continued to caress her thigh. "And what will you do for me if I satisfy you now?"

"Anything!" Playacting or not, his teasing was driving her crazy. She wanted his lips on hers, his hard maleness deep inside her.

"Then you'll use your influence to get me that piece of property?"

Her laugh was breathless. "That's what you want? Property?"

His hot gaze traveled over her so suggestively she grew moist just from his insolent perusal. "Among other things."

"Take what you want," she whispered. "All of it."

"With pleasure." His lips covered hers and he thrust forward, but his briefs prevented the joining she craved. His kiss deepened, and she moaned in frustration. He lifted his lips. "You want more?"

"You know what I want."

"It's not in the script."

"Then ad-lib."

"You're a demanding lover, Sheila." He reached beneath the comforter and tunneled his fingers through the curls at the apex of her thighs. "But I want that property," he murmured, stroking her until she gasped. "Is it mine?"

"I'll . . . try," she said, panting.

"That's not good enough." He stroked and teased. "Is it mine?"

She twisted beneath him. "Yes!"

"That's good, Sheila. Very good. Now enjoy."

She did. When the glorious spasms subsided, she gazed up at him. "Tell me it's not like that with Sheila. Not really."

He laughed softly. "Not even close. We don't have climaxes on the set."

"But sometimes . . . I bet you get aroused."

"Sometimes."

"Oh, Luke, I shouldn't have asked you to demonstrate a love scene. This isn't easy for me, thinking of you pretending to—"

"Hush, now." He reached for a cellophane package on the nightstand and quickly sheathed himself. "It's only pretend," he murmured, moving between her thighs. "This is for real." Then he drove into her, and his powerful rhythm blotted out her fears. "I love you," he whispered as she moved toward another shattering release. "I love only you."

JUST BEFORE DAWN Luke left Meg's bed and began to dress. She started to get up, but he urged her back under the comforter. "Stay there. Let me think of you lying there, dreaming of me."

"I always do. Luke, what's going to happen to us?"

"I don't know." He pulled on his briefs and reached for the flannel shirt. "I thought I could stay away from you, but two weeks later here I am, disguising myself to be with you again."

"My dad said you'd taken back your half of the farm."

"Yeah. In fact, Clint's the one who suggested I disguise myself so I could come back and check on things without stirring up the whole town. Of course, once I was here, I couldn't stay away from you."

"Well, if the disguise worked . . ."

"This time it did. And if anyone noticed the car parked in your drive, you can always make up something about an old college friend. But we can't keep that sort of thing up for too long, Meg." He pulled on the baggy jeans. "You can only have so many visiting college friends before someone thinks you're running a house of prostitution or a drug ring."

"Then I'll make trips to L.A."

"That would look suspicious, too."

Meg groaned in frustration. "I can't imagine my life without you. When you left before, I tried to resign myself to it, but I never did."

"Obviously neither did I."

"We're two intelligent people. Can't we figure out a way for this to work?"

He sat on the edge of the bed and trailed his finger down her arm. "We probably could, but how would it work in Chandler?"

"To hell with—"

"Don't say it. You don't mean it."

"When the papers reach the newsstands, my decision may be made for me. If they throw me out of Chandler, would you take me in?"

He smoothed her hair away from her face and gazed down at her. "As if you have to ask."

She laced her fingers through his. "I don't want you to go. I want to fix you breakfast. I've never done that."

He brought their joined hands to his lips and kissed her fingers one by one. "And breakfast would become lunch, and lunch would become dinner, and in between we'd make love, and I'd never go back."

Meg sighed. Slowly she relaxed her grip. "Go quickly," she said, "while I can still stand it."

14

FOR THE NEXT FEW DAYS Meg studied every strange man she saw on the street or driving down the road. One of them might be Luke, in disguise. If he did it once, he could do it again. But she knew he was back in L.A. preparing for the first week of shooting for *The Unvanquished*. He had lines to learn, costumes to be fitted. And a co-star to meet. Meg tried not to think about that. He'd convinced her that love scenes in soap operas weren't filmed in the nude. But as for love scenes in the movies, she knew better.

She had no right to be jealous. She had no right to anything involving Luke Bannister. She believed that she would see him again. They might even make love again. But their future, which neither of them wanted to face, would be a few stolen moments between long absences. Meg didn't like that idea. Once, she might have spurned it as not enough. But now she was willing to take whatever crumbs might fall her way. She couldn't renounce Luke completely. She simply wasn't that strong.

The day of the chamber meeting to elect a new president grew closer. Everyone on the chamber board talked as if she'd have no opposition, especially after the resounding success of the festival. But Meg knew that, before the vote was taken, anyone could be nominated for the position from the floor. If a scandal broke, a new nominee was sure to be put up against her. The humiliation of losing under those circumstances would be public and complete.

On Tuesday, one day before the noon board meeting on Wednesday, Clint called. "The story's been published."

Meg clutched her stomach. She'd been expecting it, but still her insides curdled. "Are you sure?"

"My buddy called me from the warehouse."

"I can't believe the timing. Tomorrow's the board meeting."

"I know, but it could be worse. My buddy's got a tight group there, and the paper won't go on the stands until Thursday. He couldn't stall much longer than that, so in a way, we're lucky it didn't show up last week."

"I guess you're right, although if it had, the suspense would be over. Did your friend say what the article looked like?"

"Just that it's on the front page. He was rushed and couldn't talk long, but he promised to hang in there for us."

"Clint, I appreciate your help."

"It's the least I can do, considering most of this mess is my fault."

"And mine."

"Hey, women never could stay away from Luke."

"And that's one of the crosses I have to bear."

"Well, I'll tell you something, Meg. He's never been serious about anybody else. Never. I quizzed him about the women he's known in L.A., and he could barely remember them. You seem to have made him forget all about them."

"That's encouraging."

"Yeah, when he showed up here the last time, all he could talk about was you. When I threatened him with bodily harm, he finally got down to business and helped me decide whether to repair one of the old harvesters or buy a new one, but his heart wasn't in it."

Meg smiled. "Thanks, Clint."

"I just wish there was some way you two could get together."

She met his comment with silence. What could she say?

"Well, I'd better get back to work. Call if you need anything. A shoulder, a beer, whatever."

"I'll do that." She hung up and stared at the phone. Everything was proceeding as planned. She'd helped manipulate things so she'd be voted in before the story came out. Except the more she thought about it, the more wrong that manipulation felt. She stared at the phone a moment longer, and before she lost her nerve, she punched in Clint's number.

He answered sounding out of breath. "Meg? I was on my way out the door. What's up?"

"I know this sounds crazy, but I'd like you to call your friend and tell him to deliver all the papers tomorrow."

"What?"

"I know you've gone to a lot of trouble to arrange this, and probably bought a few rounds of drinks for the guys after work, but I don't feel right about getting into office under false pretenses."

"Don't be an idiot, Meg! Having those papers on the stands tomorrow is like crawling under barbed wire with your fanny in the air. Don't you learn, woman?"

She sighed. "Apparently not. I told you you'd think I was out of my mind, but it has to be this way, Clint. If you want to tell me how to contact him, I'll talk to the guy."

"No, no. I'll do it. But I don't like this. And neither will Luke."

"I appreciate how hard both of you have worked to keep this quiet, but I honestly wish it had come out during the festival. At least now I'd know where I stand. Keeping secrets isn't my style. I should have realized it earlier, but I didn't."

"Boy, when Luke said you were an idealist, he wasn't kidding. I was prepared to buy all the papers we could find and put them through the shredder, but Luke said you'd never go for that."

"That's right. I wouldn't."

"Listen, you'll probably need that beer and a shoulder to cry on after the board meeting tomorrow. I've given up on the stuff for myself, but I'd be glad to pour one for you."

"Thanks, Clint. Sounds like a good offer. I'll see you then." She hung up the phone and gripped the edge of the desk. Public and complete humiliation. After tomorrow, nobody in Chandler would look at her the same way again.

She called Didi, who had known about the plan to delay the papers. She tried to talk Meg back into doing that, but Meg held firm. "Want to come over tonight?" Didi persisted. "I can throw together some pasta and break out a jug of wine. I'm not sure you should be alone to contemplate this."

"I won't be alone. I've decided to go over and tell my parents."

"Oh, my God."

"It's only fair, Didi."

"You and fair! I think the word will be inscribed on your tombstone. I wonder if the chamber deserves somebody as good as you."

Meg laughed humorlessly. "After tomorrow, I don't think people will think of me as good, Didi."

MEG TIMED HER VISIT to her parents so dinner would be finished, the dishes washed. She didn't want to have to choke down a meal during this discussion. She knocked on the kitchen door and opened it. "Mom, Dad?"

"In here, Meg," her mother called from the living room. Televised laughter indicated they were watching a sitcom.

Her father chuckled as Meg walked in. "You should watch this show, Meggie."

He hadn't called her Meggie in a long time. She wondered if it was his way of reestablishing the affectionate relationship that had eroded during the festival. Her heart ached for the camaraderie that might never exist again. Her father leaned back in his leather recliner, his face relaxed. Her mother sat on the couch with a pile of shirts that needed buttons, her new reading glasses perched on her nose.

Her mother glanced up from her sewing. "What a nice surprise, Meg." She moved the shirts aside and patted the seat next to her. "Sit down and enjoy the show."

Meg sat, feeling like the grim reaper arriving to shatter their contentment. "I'm sorry to interrupt," she said, "But I have something important to tell you."

"Oh?" Her father glanced over, a smile on his broad face from the latest joke on the screen. His smile faded as he gazed at his daughter. "What's wrong?"

"Could we turn off the TV?"

"Sure." He fumbled with the remote and the set clicked into darkness.

Meg looked at her mother, who had taken off her glasses and held them tightly in her lap. The jovial atmosphere of the room was gone, and it was Meg's fault. If only she'd had brothers and sisters, maybe this wouldn't be so hard. Maybe she wouldn't feel so responsible for their happiness.

She took a deep breath. "I need to warn you about something that will happen tomorrow. There's a tabloid that's coming out—I know you don't usually read them, but somebody will tell you about it, I'm sure—and my name and picture will be in it."

Her mother frowned. "You mean something to do with the festival?"

"No. Something to do with Luke."

Jack Hennessy snapped his recliner forward. "I saw that damned photographer running around. What did she do—rig something by superimposing your head on somebody else's body? We'll sue them, that's what we'll do. Don't worry, Meg. Nobody will believe—"

"The pictures are legitimate, Dad. I was caught coming out of Luke's hotel room at four in the morning."

Her mother gasped and her father stared at her in slack-jawed amazement.

"The photographer was waiting by the door. She took pictures of me, and then pictures of Luke coming out wearing only his jeans. Luke has just signed a contract to do a major motion picture, and his name's bigger than ever. I'm sure the story will be something about his one-night stand with the festival organizer in Chandler. And it's true."

Her father tried to speak, cleared his throat and tried again. "Couldn't...couldn't Luke have put a stop to it?"

"He tried. This was the photographer's first big break, apparently, and she wasn't about to give up her chance to advance her career."

Nora Hennessy touched her daughter's arm. "You mean everyone, not just in Chandler, but all over the country, will see this?"

"I'm afraid so, Mom. I'm sorry. I'm truly sorry. You've both tried so hard to raise a daughter who would be a credit to you, and you warned me about Luke. Now you'll have to go through the humiliation this story will bring. Neither of you deserve it."

Her father ran a shaky hand over his face. "What about you becoming president of the chamber?"

"I doubt they'll vote me in. By noon, when the board convenes, the story will probably be all over town."

He stood up and started pacing across the room. "Did the damned paper time it this way, just to ruin you?"

"No. Luke's been trying to stall them, but I guess he couldn't hold them off any longer. Clint had a link with the people who distribute the paper in Chandler, and he was going to have them hold it for a day, but I told him not to."

Her father whirled. "Well, call him back! That sounds like a reasonable plan. Get yourself into office and then deal with the story."

"No, Jack." Her mother glanced at Meg. "She wouldn't want to be voted in under those circumstances. Better to have it come out beforehand."

He continued to pace. "I'd love to get my hands on that Luke Bannister. He seduced you into going over to that hotel. Here I thought he'd changed, and it turns out he hasn't changed at all!"

"Dad, that's not what happened. Luke didn't ask me to come to his room. I sneaked over there Saturday night after the festival was over. He didn't even expect me. This is my fault, not his."

"You're always trying to protect him!"

She stood. "That's because you never understood him! Did you know his father beat him all those years after his mother died? No, I'm sure you didn't, because he never told anybody. I'm probably the only one who guessed. Luke may have seemed like a swaggering punk to you, but inside he was hurting more than any of us will ever know. It's a miracle what he's done with his life. And I . . . I love him very much."

Her father stopped pacing. Slowly he turned and faced her. "What did you say?"

"I said I love him. I was sorely tempted to leave Chandler and go back with him to L.A., but he convinced me not to. He believes in my future as a public servant and doesn't want to interfere with that."

"So instead he ruins your future?"

"That wasn't his doing! It was mine! Why can't you be angry with me?"

Slowly her father crossed the room to her. "I could never be angry with you. Don't you understand?"

"But I'm the one who's hurt you. Hurt you and Mom."

"Never mind about us."

"Your father's right." Nora came over and put her arms around Meg. "Whatever happens tomorrow, we can take it just fine. Whatever you do won't affect the price of cotton, or the sunshine in my flower garden. If some false friends snub us, we were better off without them, anyway."

Meg's eyes brimmed. "I thought you'd be devastated."

"Then I guess you don't know us as well as you thought," her mother said, hugging her.

"It's you we're worried about, Meggie." Her father patted her shoulder. "We know how much you wanted the chamber office. And if this story comes out the way you describe it, you may be out of the running."

Meg sniffed and glanced at him. "Well, then I'm out. I'll hold up my head and try again another time. After all, I come from strong stock."

"Damn right," her father said, squeezing her shoulder. "Meg Hennessy's no quitter."

"And neither are you guys," she said, her voice choked with emotion.

MEG DECIDED THE ONLY WAY she could handle the board meeting at noon the next day was if she hadn't seen the article and hadn't discussed it with anyone. She unplugged her phone before she went to bed and didn't answer her door. At eleven-thirty, dressed in a crisp, mint green linen suit, she drove to Chops Restaurant, where the chamber held its monthly board meetings in a conference room behind the main dining area.

She looked straight ahead as she walked through the restaurant and pretended not to see heads turning and comments exchanged. Whispered snippets of conversation pelted her like hailstones. ". . . looks upset . . . wouldn't have guessed . . . amazing . . . sexy . . ."

Perspiration dampened her forehead and the small of her back. No doubt about it, the word was out. The board members would know. But wasn't that what she wanted? She fought the urge to turn and run. She didn't have to go through with this. She could take her car and drive away from here, away from Chandler. Luke had said he'd take her in.

Except they hadn't thrown her out yet. If she left now, she'd be running away, quitting. If she ever expected to contribute something to the world, she needed to prove to herself that she had the backbone to take what the world dished out. She had to find out what she was made of.

She walked into the back room. Nearly every one of the eighteen board members was there, plus the ex officio members who included two people from the press and representatives from the city and the county. They'd probably gathered early to pick another nominee for president of the chamber. The procedure was simple. Her name would be presented and then nominations would be taken from the floor. No one had ever been nominated from the floor in the history of the chamber, but today would undoubtedly make history.

Conversation stopped as she walked in. She forced a smile and glanced at the one friendly face she could count on—Didi's. Didi gave her a discreet thumbs-up. Tables were arranged in a U-shape, with the current president and executive director at the bottom of the U. Meg took her seat at a chair along the side. She crossed her legs and folded her hands together to control her shaking.

Ralph Handley called the meeting to order. Meg tried to concentrate on the preliminary business—approval of the minutes, executive committee business, policy matters. She couldn't focus on any of it. She glanced around the table and noticed the edges of what must be the tabloid sticking out of briefcases and hiding under yellow legal pads. Her heart pounded as the meeting's agenda moved with maddening slowness toward the confirmation procedure.

French doors opposite her led to an area of grass and trees, both verdant with the lush green of springtime. Meg fantasized about getting up and going outdoors into the fresh air, feeling the sun on her back. A gardener was working out there, using hand clippers on a small hedge. She remembered what her mother had said—what happened today wouldn't affect the price of cotton or the sunshine on her flowers.

Meg thought about people all over the world who wouldn't give a damn what happened in this room today. Business would go forward, babies would be born, vacations would be enjoyed. And Luke. No matter what happened today, he would star in a wonderful movie and become known all over the world. She loved thinking about that, even if the idea was bittersweet, because he would inevitably move away from her.

The sound of a lawn mower startled her out of her reverie. A board member excused himself and went out to ask the gardener to move his operation away from the French doors until the meeting was over. Meg realized with a start that they were about to vote on her. Without the noise from the lawn mower, she might have been caught daydreaming at the crucial moment.

As Ralph proposed her name and asked for nominations from the floor, a sense of calm came over her. At last it would be over. Someone else would be named; someone else would be the president.

Except that no one else was nominated.

Meg glanced around the room in surprise. Her fellow board members gazed at her with interest, not condemnation. Ralph cleared his throat. "No other nominations being offered, I call for a voice vote for Meg Hennessy O'Brian as president of the chamber. All in favor, signify by saying aye."

A chorus of ayes followed.

"Nays?"

No one spoke.

"Abstentions?"

Meg struggled to find her voice. "I abstain," she croaked.

"Congratulations," Ralph said, smiling at her. "You're our new president-elect."

Meg's head buzzed. This couldn't be happening. "I don't get it." Her gaze traveled from face to face. Didi was grinning from ear to ear. "What about the story?"

"What about it?" Ralph said. "I think most of us found it charming. Good publicity for the festival, as a matter of fact."

15

CHARMING? GOOD PUBLICITY for the festival?

Meg wondered if she could be dreaming this scene. Had all the Chandler Chamber of Commerce board members read about her torrid night at the San Marcos and decided the account was "charming"? She glanced at Didi for some clue as to what was going on.

Didi met her gaze and mouthed the words "Did you read it?"

Meg shook her head.

Didi pushed back her chair. "Could we have a short recess before we finish the agenda? Five minutes?"

Ralph looked puzzled, but he nodded. Chairs scraped back and Anna Cruz, who was sitting next to Meg, leaned toward her. "Frankly, I think you missed a golden opportunity," she said with a wink.

"I'm not sure what you—"

Didi grabbed her arm and pulled her out of her chair. "Come with me, sweetie."

Meg followed Didi, who glanced around and ducked through the kitchen door with Meg in tow. She had a copy of the tabloid in her hand. When the kitchen door closed behind them, Didi shoved the paper at Meg.

There was the picture of Meg, looking disheveled and guilty, right next to the picture of Luke flying out the door wearing only his jeans. Meg steeled herself for the torrid headline, and as she read it she gasped. Lover Boy Strikes Out! Meg glanced at Didi. "Keep going."

Meg read aloud.

"'Luke Bannister, heartthrob of the hit soap *Connections* and star of the upcoming feature film *The Unvanquished*, admits he couldn't get to first base with lovely childhood sweetheart Meg O'Brian when Luke came home last month for Chandler, Arizona's annual ostrich festival. "I tried to stir up an old flame, but she wasn't impressed," Luke said. "Guess I'm not such a hot lover after all."

"'O'Brian was the organizer of the festival. Bannister says he asked for special "star" treatment, but O'Brian told him to get lost. "She came to my hotel room to discuss business and refused to let it become pleasure," Bannister said. "If this keeps happening, my reputation's going to be shot."'"

Meg folded the paper with shaking hands. "But Didi, that's not the way—"

"I was afraid that's how you'd react. Luke made himself look like a fool for you. Are you going to make his efforts wasted by calling him a liar? What sort of gratitude is that?"

"But this story isn't true!"

"It's all he could think of to help you. Let him do it, Meg."

"Do people really believe that nothing happened between us?"

"Some do, some don't. But even the ones who don't are impressed that Luke would go to such lengths to save your reputation. They're willing to let the whole thing ride."

"Didi, I don't know what to say."

"Don't say anything. Don't blow this, gal. Think of the future. Do you honestly believe that your sneaking over to the San Marcos that night is a big enough deal that it should stand in the way of your whole political career?"

"I guess not."

Didi snatched her newspaper back. "Then don't let it. Time to get back to the meeting, Madam President."

Meg followed her in a daze. True to his word, Luke had saved her. And he knew her so well that he hadn't told her his plan. He knew she would have vetoed it.

As she sat through the rest of the meeting, Meg slowly realized the enormity of what Luke had done for her. He'd sacrificed his pride. All his life he'd guarded that pride and now he'd made himself the laughingstock of the entertainment world for her. She pictured the taunts and ribbing he'd get, the comments on talk shows, the sly innuendos that Luke on screen was a far cry from Luke in person.

Even if she denied his story, she probably wouldn't be believed. His was the more believable, because it was the most outrageous. Men bragged about their conquests, not their failures. Most men. But not Luke. Not the man she loved.

After the meeting she drove to a convenience store and bought the tabloid. She didn't think her mother or father had seen it yet. They'd indicated the night before that they wouldn't dirty their hands on it, nor would they discuss the story with anyone who called. They'd be as ignorant as she had been.

Her mother was on her hands and knees in the flower garden when Meg arrived. Meg tossed the paper onto the ground next to her. Nora Hennessy stared at the large headline in silence. Then she shielded her eyes and glanced up at her daughter. "What does this mean?"

"Luke lied to save me."

Her mother picked up the paper and scrambled to her feet. Then she hurried into the kitchen to find her reading glasses. It was the first time Meg ever remembered her mother walking in from the garden without brushing off her slacks or wiping her feet. Meg followed her into the kitchen and leaned against the counter while her mother read the article, and then reread it.

At last she put the paper down on the table and took off her glasses. "So what happened at the meeting?"

"They voted me in as president."

"Did you tell them this article is wrong?"

Meg gazed at her mother. "No."

"Thank the Lord." Her mother walked over and gave Meg a hug. "You are so honest that sometimes it's ridiculous. I was afraid you'd throw what Luke did for you back in his face."

"I almost did. Didi talked me out of it."

"Let me call your father. He's out on the tractor, but he has that new cellular phone I got him for Christmas." Meg waited while she relayed the news. Her mother turned off the phone and pushed down the antenna. "He says to tell you that's wonderful, and he's so glad you showed some good sense in not spilling all the beans."

"Now I have to go find Clint." Meg picked up the paper. "He invited me over for a beer after the meeting to drown my sorrows, so I don't think he knew about this, either."

"Before you go, I have something to say." Meg paused in the door. "Once I warned you to keep straight what was fantasy and what was reality." Her mother took a deep breath. "The truth is, I don't have a lot of experience with men. Your father's been about it. I didn't realize before that some men...can make fantasies come true."

Meg swallowed the lump in her throat. "Yes, Mom, they sure can."

WHEN SHE WAS WITHIN a hundred yards of the Bannister drive, Meg noticed the rental sedan parked next to Clint's red truck. Probably just a friend, she thought, trying to stay calm. Luke wouldn't have time to flit over to Chandler today.

Still, when she parked her car behind the sedan, her heart was hammering louder than the woodpecker banging away on one of the nearby tamarisk trees. The afternoon was warm, so she left the jacket of her green suit in the car. She picked up the paper and walked around to the kitchen door, her heels crunching in the newly spread gravel. The weeds were gone.

She heard their voices through the screen door. He was here. The man she wanted to spend her life with. The man she couldn't have. She had to be upbeat, send him back to L.A. with her gratitude, but send him back, nonetheless. Perhaps they'd meet again, perhaps not. She had to accept that. She had to be strong.

The back steps smelled of new lumber and paint. She knocked on the door. Clint appeared on the other side holding a soft drink. "Took you long enough." He glanced over his shoulder. "When did you say that meeting was over? An hour ago?"

Luke's voice carried outside. "Something like that. I had enough time to get back here and shower off all the grass clippings. Lord knows what she's been doing."

Meg pushed through the door and stared at Luke sitting at the kitchen table dressed in an old T-shirt and faded jeans, with a can of cola in front of him. "You were the gardener?"

"And it's a good thing, too. I glanced through the door once and you were staring off into space just when they were about to vote on you. I started up the lawn mower, just to wake you up."

"I can't believe it. You listened in?"

"Yep." He sipped his drink. "I was driving around the restaurant wondering how to spy on the meeting, when I saw these two guys working on the landscaping. I slipped them a twenty and borrowed their equipment for an hour. That was long enough for me to hear you get elected." He paused. "Congratulations."

"But . . . but don't you have to be on the set or something?"

Luke nodded. "First thing in the morning. I begged and pleaded for the day off, and the director took pity on me. Tomorrow it's back to the salt mines."

Meg glanced at Clint and then down at the paper in her hand. "So I guess you know about this."

Clint nodded. "I do now. I didn't until this morning. I tried to call you, but no one answered."

"I unplugged the phone." She returned her attention to Luke and held up the paper. "You know I almost contradicted this at the meeting."

"I figured you might. It was worth the risk."

"Luke, you allowed everyone to think you're some sort of lecherous guy, and a dud in bed, too!"

He grinned. "Nobody's perfect."

"You shouldn't have done that, you big, crazy, foolish, lovable—"

Clint put a hand on her shoulder. "It's been a blast, but I'm outta here. The south forty needs plowing, or something. Don't expect to see me for at least three hours."

Meg turned her head in time to catch Clint's wink as he went out the kitchen door. She glanced at Luke. "I owe you a lot."

He pushed away from the table and stood. "I was hoping you'd feel that way. Real grateful."

"I am grateful."

He approached her slowly and took the paper from her hand. "Grateful women usually agree to all kinds of things."

"Anything you want."

His blue eyes sparkled as he drew her close. "This is starting to sound like one of my soap-opera scenes. Are you sure you mean 'anything'?"

"Yes." She didn't think he'd ask her to, but she would resign her office if necessary, follow him around the world, and take whatever moments of passion he had to give.

"Marry me."

"What?" She blinked in surprise. He *had* asked her to give up everything for him!

He caressed the small of her back. "Come on. You said 'anything.'"

She swallowed. Of course she wanted to marry him, no matter what the cost. "I'll tell them tomorrow that I can't serve. I'm sure there's plenty of time to—"

"Wait a minute. Who's talking about that?"

"But I can't be president of the chamber and live in L.A."

"I don't expect you to live in L.A."

"But—"

"Listen to me." He combed her hair back with his fingers. "You said once that two intelligent people should be able to work this out. I think we can. I've learned that making feature films is a lot different from the soaps. I earn more money. I can have more time off between movies. And sometimes I'll be working nearby. They're shooting part of *The Unvanquished* on location in Tubac. That's less than a three-hour drive from here."

She gazed up at him, hardly daring to believe what he was suggesting.

"And another thing. We didn't want people thinking we were shacking up during the festival, but if we got married, I can't imagine it would hurt you politically. Especially now that everyone thinks I'm a dud in the bedroom."

She laughed, unable to contain the joy bursting within her. "And I don't intend to change anybody's mind, either."

He leaned down and nipped at her earlobe. "Oh, yeah? I thought you were the one who couldn't keep secrets?"

She wrapped her arms around his neck and settled her body against his. "I'm learning that a few well-kept secrets are part of surviving in this world. I'm the only one who needs to know what a sexy guy you really are."

"What timing I have." He cupped her behind and urged her closer. "Just when you're capable of handling a secret affair, I propose marriage."

"Want to take it back?"

He tensed. "Come to think of it, you haven't officially said yes."

She savored the moment, knowing she'd remember it for the rest of her life. "Yes."

His sigh of relief was warm against her neck. He leaned back to gaze into her eyes, and his own were moist. "It'll be a crazy life."

She reached up and cradled his face in her hands. "I'm counting on that. Kiss me, loverboy."

And just like in the movies, he did.

INDULGE A LITTLE 6947 SWEEPSTAKES
NO PURCHASE NECESSARY

HERE'S HOW THE SWEEPSTAKES WORKS:
The Harlequin Reader Service shipments for January, February and March 1994 will contain, respectively, coupons for entry into three prize drawings: a trip for two to San Francisco, an Alaskan cruise for two and a trip for two to Hawaii. To be eligible for any drawing using an Entry Coupon, simply complete and mail according to directions.

There is no obligation to continue as a Reader Service subscriber to enter and be eligible for any prize drawing. You may also enter any drawing by hand printing your name and address on a 3" x 5" card and the destination of the prize you wish that entry to be considered for (i.e., San Francisco trip, Alaskan cruise or Hawaiian trip). Send your 3" x 5" entries to: Indulge a Little 6947 Sweepstakes, c/o Prize Destination you wish that entry to be considered for, P.O. Box 1315, Buffalo, NY 14269-1315, U.S.A. or Indulge a Little 6947 Sweepstakes, P.O. Box 610, Fort Erie, Ontario L2A 5X3, Canada.

To be eligible for the San Francisco trip, entries must be received by 4/30/94; for the Alaskan cruise, 5/31/94; and the Hawaiian trip, 6/30/94. No responsibility is assumed for lost, late or misdirected mail. Sweepstakes open to residents of the U.S. (except Puerto Rico) and Canada, 18 years of age or older. All applicable laws and regulations apply. Sweepstakes void wherever prohibited.

For a copy of the Official Rules, send a self-addressed, stamped envelope (WA residents need not affix return postage) to: Indulge a Little 6947 Rules, P.O. Box 4631, Blair, NE 68009, U.S.A.

INDR93

INDULGE A LITTLE 6947 SWEEPSTAKES
NO PURCHASE NECESSARY

HERE'S HOW THE SWEEPSTAKES WORKS:
The Harlequin Reader Service shipments for January, February and March 1994 will contain, respectively, coupons for entry into three prize drawings: a trip for two to San Francisco, an Alaskan cruise for two and a trip for two to Hawaii. To be eligible for any drawing using an Entry Coupon, simply complete and mail according to directions.

There is no obligation to continue as a Reader Service subscriber to enter and be eligible for any prize drawing. You may also enter any drawing by hand printing your name and address on a 3" x 5" card and the destination of the prize you wish that entry to be considered for (i.e., San Francisco trip, Alaskan cruise or Hawaiian trip). Send your 3" x 5" entries to: Indulge a Little 6947 Sweepstakes, c/o Prize Destination you wish that entry to be considered for, P.O. Box 1315, Buffalo, NY 14269-1315, U.S.A. or Indulge a Little 6947 Sweepstakes, P.O. Box 610, Fort Erie, Ontario L2A 5X3, Canada.

To be eligible for the San Francisco trip, entries must be received by 4/30/94; for the Alaskan cruise, 5/31/94; and the Hawaiian trip, 6/30/94. No responsibility is assumed for lost, late or misdirected mail. Sweepstakes open to residents of the U.S. (except Puerto Rico) and Canada, 18 years of age or older. All applicable laws and regulations apply. Sweepstakes void wherever prohibited.

For a copy of the Official Rules, send a self-addressed, stamped envelope (WA residents need not affix return postage) to: Indulge a Little 6947 Rules, P.O. Box 4631, Blair, NE 68009, U.S.A.

INDR93

INDULGE A LITTLE
SWEEPSTAKES

OFFICIAL ENTRY COUPON

This entry must be received by: APRIL 30, 1994
This month's winner will be notified by: MAY 15, 1994
Trip must be taken between: JUNE 30, 1994-JUNE 30, 1995

YES, I want to win the San Francisco vacation for two. I understand that the prize includes round-trip airfare, first-class hotel, rental car and pocket money as revealed on the "wallet" scratch-off card.

Name________________________________

Address ____________________ Apt. ____________

City________________________________

State/Prov.________________ Zip/Postal Code____________

Daytime phone number________________________
(Area Code)

Account #________________________________

Return entries with invoice in envelope provided. Each book in this shipment has two entry coupons—and the more coupons you enter, the better your chances of winning!

© 1993 HARLEQUIN ENTERPRISES LTD. MONTH1